The Watcher of Windcliff

THE
WATCHER
OF
WINDCLIFF

J.H. Rhodes

47N⬤RTH

Text Copyright © 1980 by J. H. Rhodes

Published by 47North
P.O. Box 400818
Las Vegas, NV 89140

ISBN-13: 9781477837740
ISBN-10: 1477837744

The Watcher of Windcliff

CHAPTER ONE

Marcia Carpenter stood watching from the edge of the rocky promontory as Teal Island began to shed the vestiges of the morning mist. Above her, gulls wheeled and cried as they rode the currents of air. Before long the Maine fog would dissipate and Teal Island would become clearer, with the house, Windcliff, revealed against the far horizon. To Marcia seeing Windcliff emerging from the mist was like something out of a fairy tale or Sir Walter Scott.

How many mornings had she stood on that same spot, never tiring of the view, always wondering what Windcliff looked like on the inside?

Below her, angry waves crashed with a deafening roar against the rockbound coast, sending white spume high into the crisp morning air.

The sea frightened Marcia. She had been afraid of it ever since it had claimed the life of her father ten years before when his small fishing boat had capsized. Her father had been a good swimmer, but he had struck his head on something and had drowned. Marcia's mother had been grief-stricken, but she was a strong-willed person and had managed to provide her daughter with a great deal of love if not worldly possessions. When she had passed on last year, Marcia at twenty realized she had inherited her mother's strong character.

1

After graduating high school, Marcia had found a job in Adam Long's law office right in her hometown of Penwick. She could type and take dictation and had a genuine interest in helping people.

Adam Long was twenty years older than Marcia and she regarded him as a sort of big brother. However, his feelings for her had gradually become somewhat more than brotherly.

He had asked her out to dinner the previous evening. They had dined at a seafood restaurant that served delicious lobster. It was during the course of the evening that Adam had revealed his true feelings to her.

"I don't have to tell you that I've always been very pleased with your work, Marcia," he had said, the candle flame flickering against his salt-and-pepper hair. Adam Long was still a handsome man, which Marcia thought was to his credit. "As a matter of fact, I'm quite pleased with everything I see about you."

Marcia had felt her face redden. She hoped he wouldn't see it in the dimly lit room.

"You are a very beautiful young woman," Adam had gone on. "Such lustrous hair, such lively eyes." Then he praised all her other features.

Marcia had never considered herself beautiful. Her light brown hair, which she wore in a short, fluffy cut, was average in color. She had her mother's fair complexion, with her father's merry, mischievous brown eyes, slightly flecked with gold. Her nose was a trifle too long, but she was satisfied with her mouth, not to mention her trim figure, which she took for granted.

All the while that Adam Long talked, she couldn't keep her mind on what he was saying. For some reason, Gregg Spaniard kept slipping into her thoughts. She had fallen hopelessly in love with Gregg from the first moment she had seen him walking along the narrow streets of Penwick.

The Spaniards, old Joshia and his son Gregg, owned Teal Island. To the people of Penwick they were as remote as the island itself. Gregg had attended school at Penwick, three grades ahead of Marcia, then had gone off to Europe to further his education. They had never once spoken, and Marcia was certain that Gregg did not even know she existed. Still, she could not rid herself of that strange excited feeling she always got when she saw him or heard his name mentioned.

Each morning as Marcia stood watching for the appearance of Windcliff, she dreamed of seeing the inside of that mysterious mansion. It was her escape from the mundane life she lived in the small but neat apartment not far from Penwick Bay. At the moment, Marcia had no friends of her own age. They had scattered after high school, moving from the restrictive environs of the small town. The only person she knew in the apartment building was Clarita Hooper.

Clarita was a real character—tall, ramrod straight, with iron-gray hair cut short, not one strand ever out of place. Clarita with the ever-present binoculars dangling from the leather strap about her neck.

Once Marcia had asked her why she was never without the binoculars.

Clarita gave her an imperious look. "Why, I'm a bird watcher. My late husband gave me these binoculars. Although he wasn't as curious a person as I."

Marcia had the feeling that birds weren't the only things Clarita watched through the binoculars. It became clear to Marcia that Clarita Hooper was a busybody who knew everything that went on in the apartment complex where they both lived. Because of this, Marcia was polite to the tall woman but kept her distance, although it wasn't easy to ignore Clarita Hooper.

"I don't believe you've been listening to a thing I've been saying!" Adam Long's voice had brought Marcia abruptly back to the present.

Marcia flashed an embarrassed smile at him and took a sip of coffee. "I'm sorry, Adam, my mind was a thousand miles away."

"That's quite a distance. I must be losing my touch," Adam said wryly.

"Would you mind repeating what you just said?" Marcia asked.

"Some other time. When I have your undivided attention."

At that moment Adam glanced past Marcia, his face registering the intense look it got when he became absorbed in business.

"Would you excuse me for a few minutes, Marcia? I see one of my clients that I've been trying to reach for days. How fortunate I happened to run into him here."

When Adam had gone, Marcia glanced into the wall-length mirror that hung in front of her. She watched as Adam threaded his way through the crowded tables until he came to a solitary figure who was dining alone. Marcia's pulse quickened. Adam had stopped at a table where Gregg Spaniard sat.

Marcia could not take her eyes off the handsome, dark-haired Gregg Spaniard whose jutting chin seemed even more pronounced as he listened intently to what Adam was saying. She quickly turned her attention to her coffee but found her eyes straying back to the mirror. Even in the dimly lighted restaurant

Gregg Spaniard's good looks could not be ignored.

Once Gregg glanced casually into the mirror and for a moment their eyes met. Marcia quickly looked down at the table. She reached for her glass of water and almost spilled it as she raised it to her lips. Then, as though magnetized by the mirror, she found herself staring at it again. Luckily, Gregg had directed his interest to what Adam was saying.

When Adam returned, he sat down briskly. "If you don't mind, Marcia, I'll take you home. I have some work to do at the office."

"Does that work have anything to do with the Spaniard estate?" Marcia asked.

"That was pretty obvious, wasn't it?" Adam said. "Yes, as a matter of fact, my conversation with Gregg was about some legal matters that require his signature."

Marcia's interest quickened. "But I thought Joshia Spaniard was still the head of the family. Shouldn't he be the one to sign anything in connection with Windcliff?"

Adam didn't appear to be perturbed over Marcia's question. "Joshia Spaniard had a stroke a few weeks ago. It left him speechless and bedridden. Fortunately, he had turned all legal matters over to Gregg a few months ago. So Gregg already had legal authority to sign for Joshia. Hadn't you heard about Joshia's illness?"

Marcia shook her head. "I'm sure that if the word had gotten around, Clarita Hooper would be the first to know. Does Mr. Spaniard have anyone to take care of him?"

"Gregg mentioned something about a nurse. But she's expected to leave, so he'll have to find a replacement."

Marcia couldn't help glancing over Adam's shoulder into the mirror once more, but Gregg Spaniard was gone. A young couple had taken his place at the table. Idly Marcia wondered if Gregg was now on his way back to Teal Island and Windcliff.

"You've lived here all your life, Marcia," Adam said, snapping her attention away from the mirror. "Whatever became of Gregg's mother?"

"She ran off with another man," Marcia told him. "An artist who had come to Windcliff to do her portrait. From what I gather, Joshia Spaniard divorced her and got custody of Gregg. Joshia never remarried, so he must have loved his wife very much in spite of the divorce."

"Or became so bitter that he didn't want to get married again," Adam said. It was not so much the cynical remark that Adam made but rather the mocking look in his eyes that sent a chill down Marcia's spine. Beneath Adam Long's civilized appearance, there was a smug streak that turned Marcia off. Adam Long had a lot of charm, but at times it seemed he cared very little for people and their problems.

Once she had overheard him speaking to a visiting lawyer in his office. "Thank God people get themselves into all sorts of scrapes," he had said. "If it wasn't for that, neither one of us would have an income."

That remark had shocked Marcia. Surely all lawyers did not feel that way about their clients. Marcia had chosen to believe that Adam Long was in a bad mood when he said that.

"Shall we go?" Adam said now, getting to his feet.

Marcia was quiet all the way home to her apartment. She was thinking about Gregg and old Joshia Spaniard. Life for the only son of such a wealthy man must be very lonely in that huge house in the bay. And growing up without a mother must have been even lonelier. She felt lucky that she had had her mother to take care of her while she was growing up.

In a way, Gregg and Marcia were somewhat alike, with similar backgrounds. Gregg had been raised by one parent, his father, while she had had only her mother to care for her. Marcia dismissed that thought. She had loved her mother deeply, but there had been times when she had missed her father while she was growing up.

When they reached her apartment, Adam leaned forward to kiss her, but Marcia turned her head so that the kiss landed on her cheek.

Adam merely shrugged as she hastily slipped out of the car. "There'll be other times," he said. "See you tomorrow, Marcia."

With that Adam pulled away, leaving Marcia staring at the sleek departing luxury car.

Marcia turned to enter her apartment house, but she felt restless and thought a brief walk might help her to sleep, to clear the thoughts from her mind. It was only a short distance to the sea, and beyond, Windcliff.

The night was cool, but Marcia was used to that. Ahead of her she could hear the restless surging of the tide as it crashed upon the rocky shore. She stood watching the distant lights in the mansion that seemed to hover above the moon-drenched sea.

As she stood there, Marcia saw the lights of a small vessel as it headed in the direction of Teal Island. Could that boat possibly be manned by Gregg Spaniard? she wondered idly.

At the thought of Gregg, her pulse quickened. The memory of seeing him in the restaurant rushed over her like the dark waters of the sea below her. She stood there until the lights of the small craft disappeared into a cove of the island.

Then she returned to her apartment. She could not help noticing that Clarita Hooper's door closed just as she opened her own. Marcia shook her head and with an amused sigh went inside.

She changed into her pajamas and climbed into bed. As she lay there she thought about Adam Long. He had made his intentions fairly clear that evening. But Marcia was not interested in the handsome lawyer. She would have to find a way of telling him so, without hurting his feelings. Otherwise her job at Adam's office would be intolerable. And she liked working there. Besides, jobs were not all that easy to come by in Penwick.

If she kept this up, Marcia thought, she wouldn't get any sleep that night. So she reached for a book she kept on the nightstand and lost herself in its pages until her eyes became heavy. Then she turned off the light and soon drifted off to sleep.

As usual, her dreams were of Windcliff and the sea. Marcia found herself crossing the bay in a small boat, the sea threatening to capsize it at any moment. When she reached the shore of Teal Island, there was a path that led to the house. A violent wind had arisen and Marcia fought the gale until she reached the door of Windcliff. She pounded on the door, begging to be let in, but no one answered her pleading.

She awoke abruptly to the shrill ringing of the telephone. It was still dark outside and Marcia stumbled to the living room, where the phone stood on a small table.

"Hello," she said, still not quite awake.

"This is Adam. Sorry to call you at this hour of the night, but it's urgent."

"What is it, Adam?" Marcia asked.

"I'll be leaving first thing in the morning for New

York on business and I wanted to ask a favor of you. Would you take some papers to Windcliff tomorrow for me? They require Gregg's signature."

Windcliff! Marcia couldn't believe what she was hearing. She fought to keep the excitement from her voice as she told Adam she would be happy to run his errand.

"There will be a boat waiting for you at about two o'clock. Gregg has arranged for it. Once the papers are signed, keep them in the office until I return."

"When will that be?" Marcia asked.

"Tomorrow is Friday. I don't expect to return until next weekend. When I do, we'll continue with our discussion of last night."

Marcia wasn't too happy to hear that news and she was glad when Adam hung up. But not before he told her where the important documents were kept and where she should return them. Adam Long was a methodical man.

It was a good thing that Marcia had gotten a few hours' sleep before the call came from Adam. When she went back to bed, she tossed and turned, and finally when the first light of morning came she got dressed and had a cup of coffee.

Now Marcia stood on the cliff looking toward Teal Island. In a matter of minutes Adam Long had made it possible for her dream to be realized. In a few hours she would be aboard the craft that would take her across Penwick Bay to Windcliff. She couldn't help feeling that all this might just possibly be a dream, a dream that would end with a rude awakening in her apartment. She even went so far as to pinch herself. The pain was real, just as real as what was soon to happen to her.

As she stood there, high on the windswept cliffs, the

morning fog continued to lift and the rocky shores of Teal Island became clearer and clearer. Then slowly the vaporous mist drifted upward from Windcliff.

She saw the house standing proudly, remotely, in the center of the island. Then, as she watched, the fog once again grew thicker and the house was lost to her.

Marcia turned and walked along the winding pathway. A shiver swept over her for no reason. Or was there a reason? she wondered.

CHAPTER TWO

At the office that afternoon Marcia located the documents in the place Adam had described. The office was a small one, in keeping with the small-town atmosphere of Penwick. The only two people who ordinarily occupied the building were Adam and herself. Adam's office was to the right of her desk, and his door was usually open. In spite of the small size of the town, Adam did a remarkable business. Some of his clients were from out of the state and Marcia concluded that these well-paying clients accounted for Adam's huge ten-room house on the outskirts of Penwick.

There were times when Marcia wondered why Adam had remained a bachelor for so long. He was attractive, a meticulous dresser, generous, and quite mannerly. Perhaps he had been too busy building up his list of clients to ever seriously consider marriage. That could have been the reason. Marcia hoped that someday he would find the right woman. Although Adam was attentive, she could not see herself as his wife. In a way she dreaded the confrontation with him when he returned from New York.

Carefully stuffing the papers in a sleek leather folder, she closed the zipper and gave the office a quick, critical look. The few plants had been watered and the filing cabinets were all securely locked, as were all the windows.

"You're only going to be gone for a few hours," Marcia said aloud. "Why all this extra attention?"

Having reassured herself that everything was in order, she closed the front door and locked it. There was no need to drive her car that short distance to the bay—although, as she glanced at the sky, she saw that gray clouds had begun to gather in the west and the air held a hint of rain. For an instant she thought about returning to her apartment for a raincoat.

But that would only mean she might be confronted by Clarita Hooper. Clarita wouldn't hesitate to ask where she was going. Marcia did not feel up to a question-and-answer session with Clarita. It was better if she just went to Windcliff without anyone knowing her destination.

As she walked toward the bay, it suddenly dawned on her that there were so few people whom she actually could call close friends. Of course, growing up in Penwick, she knew all the shopkeepers and most of the population. But they were only acquaintances, not what one would call true friends. In school she had been close to Avis Trent and several other girls, but Avis was away at college now. And the others had moved to Boston or New York. Marcia made a mental note to write Avis when she returned from Windcliff.

Thinking of Windcliff and the certainty that before long she would actually be stepping inside the house of her dreams gave Marcia a strange feeling in the pit of her stomach. It was still hard for her to realize that what she had longed for, for so many years, was about to become a reality.

Leaving the familiar street behind her, Marcia took a narrow pathway that led to the jetty, the only wharf in Penwick Bay. It was odd that Gregg Spaniard's boat last night hadn't appeared to come from the jetty. Perhaps in the darkness she had gotten her directions confused. Somehow the craft had appeared to be moving from the far shore, a great distance from the jetty. That stretch of land held any number of small coves where a boat might be anchored, although it was dangerous to moor a craft in any of these coves as the tides were strong and unpredictable.

These thoughts were suddenly gone from Marcia's mind when she saw the runabout with the outboard motor waiting at the end of the jetty.

As she neared the boat, a man who had been sitting on a flat rock turned in her direction. He was heavyset with greasy brown hair and narrow, close-set eyes. There was a faint scar on his right cheek that ran in a jagged line from below his right eye to the corner of his mouth. Marcia had never seen the man before. In a town the size of Penwick a stranger stood out like a sore thumb.

He got to his feet when Marcia approached and she could see that his clothes were rumpled and unkempt, as though he had been sleeping in them.

"You Marcia Carpenter?" he said in a low, raspy voice.

Marcia was so taken aback that she could only nod her head.

"Get in. I have orders to take you to Teal Island. There's a storm on its way and I don't want to be caught out there when it hits," the man said, not offering to help her in any way.

With some difficulty Marcia managed to climb aboard the small vessel and take a seat. The man's surly attitude at first had frightened her. Now she was becoming angry at his ill manners. Marcia sat with the leather folder across her lap and one hand on the damp, brine-soaked railing. Her guide cast off, and the motor sputtered and roared to life. The boat pulled quickly away from the jetty and Marcia cast an apprehensive look at the receding coastline.

She tried not to glance at the angry waves that surged up to the small boat in front. If she did, she knew that the terror which lay in the back of her mind would suddenly wash over her. Instead, she sat rigid, looking at the foaming water churned up in the wake of the boat. She prayed that the crossing of the bay would be uneventful and swift.

Her surly guide sat behind her and she could feel his beady eyes now and then focused upon the back of her head.

There was no use in not being friendly, Marcia thought. Perhaps she had misjudged the man.

"Have you been with the Spaniards long?" she asked.

"No," came the grudging response. The man was anything but garrulous.

Marcia was not to be put off. "You're not from Pen wick, are you?"

The man made a snarling noise. "Hardly. I'm from Los Angeles."

"Then you're a long way from home," Marcia said.

"You might say that," the man said, and there was a mocking quality in his voice.

"You know my name. But what do they call you?" Marcia persisted.

"Joe's good enough," was the response.

It was evident that Joe, if that was his real name, had no intention of telling Marcia what his last name was. She was surprised that he had even told her he was from California. From Los Angeles to Penwick was quite a distance. And from the beat-up look of Joe's face the trip between the two cities had not been a pleasant one.

As the boat neared the halfway point between the mainland and Teal Island, the sun went behind a dark cloud. The waters of the bay turned a slate gray. There was always a wind blowing in from the Atlantic, but its velocity had suddenly increased. A few scattered drops of rain began to fall. Marcia put her arms around herself, regretting now that she hadn't taken the time to get her raincoat from the apartment.

Without a word Joe tossed a yellow slicker to her, and she slipped it on, thanking him, but his attention had returned to navigating the runabout.

Seeing the churning water and the angry whitecaps, Marcia became more and more terrified. What if something happened to the boat? It appeared to be so frail out here in the wild waters. She could not swim. Ever since the accident that took her father's life she had been too frightened to go into the water.

"You ain't scared, are you?" came Joe's scratchy voice. "This boat has seen lots of worse storms than this."

Joe's words were not reassuring. If anything, he was almost making fun of her. When they reached Teal Island, she would have a word with Gregg Spaniard about his hired help. Then she thought better of that. After all, there was only one way to return to the mainland and that would have to be in a boat. She would hate to think of herself at the mercy of Joe if he were angry at her for complaining to his employer.

Suddenly this whole adventure had lost its appeal. Marcia would have given anything at that moment to be back in Penwick, in the nice cozy office. Even the prospect of seeing the interior of Windcliff no longer interested her. All she could think of was getting safely out of the boat onto firm land.

By the time they were close to Teal Island, the rain was falling in a steady downpour. Joe guided the runabout into a sheltered cove and Marcia managed to get ashore.

"How do we get to Windcliff?" Marcia asked, slipping the folder of documents beneath the slicker.

"Follow me," Joe said as he began walking up a narrow pathway between rain-splattered rocks.

Marcia had to hurry in order to keep up with the squat man. She did not want to lose sight of him for fear of losing her way on the unfamiliar island. Several times she slipped and had to reach out with her free hand to keep from falling. Once Joe turned to stare at her as she tried desperately to keep from losing her footing. She could not be certain, but she thought she detected a fiendish grin on his face.

The path went through a clump of boulders, behind which Joe disappeared. Marcia staggered along the pathway, half falling in the mud created by the downpour.

When she reached the end of the boulders, she still could not see Joe anywhere.

Frantically, Marcia called his name. But her voice was lost in the pelting rain. Panic seized her and she began to run. The rain got into her eyes, and the thorny shrubbery that lined the pathway stung her ankles. She could hear her heart pounding in her ears, and her breath was like a sharp knife in her lungs.

Ahead of her, on the highest part of the island, she could see lights. That had to be Windcliff, she thought. She had to keep those lights in view, like the beacon of a lighthouse in a stormy sea.

Gusts of wind lashed at Marcia as though the very

elements were trying to drive her away from the island. Marcia raced onward, the wind driving near-blinding rain against her face. At one point the path branched off to a second pathway. Marcia was confused. Which trail would lead her to the safety of Windcliff? She decided to stay on the path she had been following. Somehow it appeared to head in the direction of the lights.

A powerful gust of wind caught her unexpectedly and she lost her balance, sprawling in the oozy, slick mud. As she went down, she instinctively used both hands to break the fall, and the folder fell from the slicker, making a dull thud as it plopped in the muddy lane.

Crawling on her hands and knees, Marcia fumbled in the mud until she found the folder. Thank heavens she had had the foresight to put the documents in a watertight container. Getting to her feet, Marcia shielded her eyes with a hand against the pelting rain. In the distance she could see the faint glow of lights. Windcliff could not be far away.

But would the house welcome her? The memory of the last dream she had had returned vividly to her. As in that dream, she was battling the forces of nature to reach the safety of the house.

Renewed strength flowed through Marcia's body as she stared at the spectral lights of the house. Determined that she would not be beaten by the storm, and by Joe's obvious efforts to abandon her, she moved toward Windcliff.

There were a few scattered trees, bent from the constant buffeting of the wind, ahead of her. Summoning all her strength, she made a dash for one of them and leaned against its gnarled trunk. Here she was temporarily sheltered from the onslaught of the storm. Hunched against the wet bark of the tree, Marcia took a few minutes to get her breath.

Below her, the island sloped to its rocky cliffs. It was difficult to realize that she had traveled such a short distance. It seemed to Marcia that she had been walking for hours and had covered a great deal of ground. When, in reality, she had only been walking a relatively short way.

She wondered what Adam's reaction would be when she told him what had befallen her. Would he be angered? Or would he merely be amused by it all? She had no way of proving that Joe had abandoned her. Perhaps he hadn't. Perhaps it was just her imagination working overtime. He might at this very moment be searching for her. Marcia thought about calling out to him, shouting his name. But with the fury of the wind, it would be useless to do so.

Now that she had caught her breath, she decided to attempt to reach the house. The yellowish glow from the lights appeared to be nearer from where she stood.

Reluctantly, Marcia left the shelter of the tree. At once the wind blasted her, showering her with chilly, stinging rain. Now that she was so close to her destination, the slashing wind was not as fearsome as it had been earlier.

The trail had widened now and eventually gave way to a gravelly area. It couldn't be a driveway, Marcia reasoned. What on earth would the Spaniards do with a car? There was absolutely nowhere to drive, and walking seemed the only sensible means of getting around Teal Island. She wondered if Gregg knew how to drive. Surely he did, even though there would be no opportunity for him to drive on the island.

The gravelly area curved to the right of the house, leaving a wide, grassy lawn fronting the two-storied structure. Marcia could now make out the white pillars that stood wraithlike in the driving rain. There were balconies for the rooms in the upper portion of the house. And they all had wrought-iron railings that gave off a faint lustrous reflection from the light coming from the windows below.

Marcia stumbled onto the wide front porch, out of the biting force of the wind. She stood there for a moment taking in her surroundings. Although the house was quite old, it was in excellent condition. Anyway, the outside was in good shape.

Glancing across the island, she could hardly see beyond the wide, sprawling front lawn. The rain was like a curtain that had been dropped by some unseen hand. It was so dark she could have mistaken the time for evening, although she knew it was only late in the afternoon.

A shiver went through Marcia and she realized that her shoes were soaking wet as well as her hair and whatever part of her cotton dress the slicker did not cover. She turned and hurried toward the entrance. There was a huge ancient knocker in the design of a Spanish galleon in the center of a heavy oak door.

As Marcia raised the knocker and let it fall, the dream once more came back to her. In her dream she had pounded on the door but there had been no answer. Now, as in that haunting dream, she waited.

CHAPTER THREE

Finally—unlike the situation in Marcia's dream—the door to Windcliff was flung open. The glare of blinding light forced Marcia to blink. Then a shadow fell between her and the light.

"You must be the girl with the documents," said a male voice, and Marcia found herself looking into the steel-blue eyes of a stranger whose blond hair shimmered in the light coming from behind him.

"I'm Marcia Carpenter," she said, wondering how long she would be forced to stand outside. "Somehow Joe and I got separated in the storm. I had to find the house on my own."

"Please come in," said the stranger as he stepped aside.

Marcia hesitantly took her first step into Windcliff. It was not the way she had so often dreamed it would be. She had not envisioned herself looking like a drowned rat on this longed-for visit.

"Let me take your slicker. Then let's go into the library. There's a nice warm fire on the hearth."

Marcia hesitated once more. She did not know this person who offered her such hospitality. The stranger must have sensed her apprehension.

"I'm Brock Janis. Gregg is my cousin. Now that the formalities are over and done with, may I help you out of that rain-drenched slicker?"

"Please," Marcia said, feeling a flush of color redden her cheeks. "I must look a mess."

Brock Janis arched an appraising eyebrow. "A very becoming mess," he said, making Marcia feel even more uncomfortable.

While Brock Janis took off her slicker and walked over to a closet to hang it up, she got her first look at the interior of Windcliff. She found herself in a wide, high-ceilinged hall. Along the walls were paintings of seascapes, and at the far right end was a circular staircase leading to the second floor.

There were four doors branching off the hall. Through the one nearest her, she could see the book-lined library. And at the far end of the hall, just off the staircase, she glimpsed a dining room. Across from the dining room was another door, which was shut. The door to her right was also closed, so she had no idea where it might lead.

Marcia could not believe that she was actually inside Windcliff. But it was true, and she had to admit to herself that it lived up to her expectations. Damp and rain-soaked though she was, she still felt like a princess who had been invited to a ball in a royal palace.

Her reverie was interrupted as Brock Janis returned from hanging up her slicker.

He was tall and fairly slender, but there was a strength about him that his flashy clothes could not disguise. It was his clothing that puzzled Marcia. Gregg had always had impeccable taste. His clothes were conservative in cut and color, while his cousin wore loud, bright apparel that could have knocked her eyes out.

Brock led her through the open door of the library where flames crackled invitingly in the fireplace.

"Would you care for a brandy? Or a cup of coffee?" her host asked.

"Coffee would be wonderful," Marcia said, clutching the folder of documents.

When Brock excused himself in order to bring her coffee, Marcia took a seat by the fireplace. The warmth of the blazing logs felt good, and she was tempted to remove her shoes to dry off her damp feet. Now that she was sitting down, she placed the folder next to her chair where she could keep an eye on it and it would not be so obvious.

Glancing above the fireplace mantel, she saw a portrait of a man in formal attire. It was Joshia Spaniard painted several years ago. The resemblance between Gregg and his father was startling. If she had wanted to peek into the future and glimpse Gregg as he might look when he was older, she couldn't have been given a better opportunity.

Thinking of Gregg, Marcia wondered where he might be. It was odd that Brock Janis had met her at the door and not Gregg. But then she remembered what Adam had told her about Joshia's sudden illness. Maybe Gregg was with his dad.

Looking at the portrait, Marcia recalled the times she had seen Joshia Spaniard strolling purposefully through Penwick. His hair had been a snowy white mane, but he carried himself straight as a ramrod. How sad it was to think of all that vitality suddenly being struck down.

She was so lost in her thoughts that she jumped when Brock returned and said, "I see you are admiring the admiral's portrait. A very good likeness, don't you agree?"

Marcia turned to face Brock. "Admiral? Are you referring to Mr. Spaniard?"

Brock offered her a cup of coffee. "Who else? We've always called the old man admiral."

"I wasn't aware that he was ever in the navy," Marcia said, sipping the hot, warming liquid.

A sudden scowl crossed Brock's face, disappearing almost at once. But not before Marcia had seen the quick change in his expression.

"Of course, he wasn't in the navy. That was just a name the family gave him. I suppose it came about with him living so close to the sea."

Brock settled himself on the sofa not far from Marcia. He took a sip from a brandy snifter on the little table right next to the sofa. Marcia noted that the glass was almost filled to the brim. It was evident that Gregg's cousin liked his liquor.

"When did you arrive at Teal Island?" Marcia asked, grasping at any topic for conversation.

"Last night. Shortly before Gregg got the urgent call from Boston," Brock said, holding the brandy snifter up against the firelight, examining the amber liquid.

"Boston! But Mr. Long told me that Gregg—Mr. Spaniard—would be here to sign these documents."

"It was all quite sudden," Brock's voice droned on. "You may leave the papers with us. I'll see that they are signed when Gregg returns."

"When do you expect him back?" Marcia asked, surprised at the turn of events.

Brock shrugged. "Tomorrow perhaps. Or even later."

Marcia did not like leaving the papers with Brock Janis. Something in his manner was very disturbing to her. Somehow she could not trust Gregg's cousin.

At that moment Marcia sneezed. Brock put down the glass of brandy.

"One thing is certain. You have to get out of those wet clothes. And you certainly can't return to the mainland while this storm is raging."

Marcia could not help but gasp when Brock mentioned her damp clothing.

"Oh, don't look so shocked," Brock said with a mischievous glint in his eyes. "Evie is just about your size. I'm sure she'll be able to find something for you to wear."

"Who is Evie? The new nurse?" Marcia wanted to know.

"Nurse! That's a good one!" Brock was beginning to show the effects of the brandy. "Evie Andrews is my fiancee. She came along with me when I decided to visit Windcliff. Besides, it would be a good opportunity for her to meet the family."

Although Brock appeared to be in a jovial mood, Marcia could not help but notice how his steely blue eyes did not show any merriment.

"Where is Miss Andrews?" Marcia asked, anxious now to keep Brock's mind occupied.

"She's with the admiral. He doesn't require much attention, but Evie has had a little medical training. So she's putting it to the test."

Marcia took a last swallow of coffee. It was cold now and bitter tasting.

"Then I gather the other nurse has left the island."

Brock nodded.

"She went ashore last night with Gregg. From what I have been told, another nurse will be arriving in a few days. There was some sort of mix-up. Anyway, Evie volunteered to look after the admiral until the replacement arrived."

Marcia wondered how ill Joshia was if he could be left in the hands of a relative stranger until a qualified nurse became available. She wondered what Evie Andrews looked like and what sort of person she was. She hadn't long to ponder this question for at that moment a young woman walked into the library.

Evie Andrews was about Marcia's height and size. Her hair was a flashy orange color, and she would have been pretty if she had scraped away the layers of makeup on her face.

"Ah, Evie. Our guest has arrived. Marcia Carpenter, this is my fiancee, Evie Andrews," Brock said, getting to his feet.

Evie walked deliberately over to where Brock stood and linked an arm through his. The gesture was very obvious. Evie Andrews was making it clear that Brock belonged to her, so hands off. As far as Marcia was concerned, Evie could have Brock Janis and be welcome to him.

"Hello, Marcia. You sure picked a lousy time to come to visit," Evie said with a haughty toss of her orange hair.

"This isn't a social call," Marcia replied. "I work for Adam Long, the lawyer. He asked me to deliver some paper for Gregg Spaniard's signature."

At the mention of Gregg's name, Marcia detected a slight nervous widening in Evie's eyes. Evie turned to face Brock, who gave her an impassive look.

"I've told Miss Carpenter about Gregg," he said. "How he was called away on business. To Boston."

Evie turned her attention back to Marcia. "That's right. He left in kind of a hurry last night."

"How is Gregg's father?" Marcia asked, meeting Evie's glacial look levelly.

"The admiral? Oh, he's just dandy. Not much I can do for him. He's flat on his back and can't say a word. But he's a sweet old codger, in his way."

For someone who would eventually become a part of the Spaniard family, Evie Andrews did not appear to be too sympathetic toward Joshia Spaniard. But, Marcia figured, she mustn't judge Evie Andrews by first impressions.

"Miss Carpenter will be staying for the night," Brock said and Marcia began to protest.

"The storm isn't about to let up," he added, silencing her with a look. "You might as well convince yourself that you are staying for the night. There are plenty of rooms, so don't let that worry you."

"You can say that again," Evie said with a smirk. "The old place should be called the Teal Hilton for unpaying guests."

With that comment both Evie and Brock broke into gales of laughter. Somehow Marcia did not see the humor in the remark and considered it in poor taste. It was almost impossible for Marcia to believe that Gregg was related to such an uncouth man as Brock Janis. And Evie was no better than Brock.

"Run along, Evie, and take Marcia with you. See if you can find her something to change into."

Evie arched a cynical eyebrow. "So it's Marcia now, is it?"

Brock's face became hard and a deadly hint of anger flared in his cold eyes. "As long as Marcia is staying over, I think we can dispense with formalities."

Evie whirled and glared at Marcia. And her eyes were filled with dislike.

"I think I can find something that might fit you. Only, it probably will be a little snug," she said tartly.

Ignoring the remark, Marcia followed obediently in Evie's wake. The last thing she wanted to do was to have a confrontation with this woman, especially now that she would have to remain in the house overnight.

Evie walked swiftly across the wide hall toward the circular staircase. Evidently all the bedrooms were on the second floor. Marcia found herself staring once more at the enormous seascapes. Then she lengthened her stride to catch up with Evie.

At the top of the stairs was a narrow, dimly lit hallway that led to a longer, wider hallway. Here Marcia saw there were six rooms. Evie went directly to her own room, with Marcia following reluctantly.

Evie's room was a mess—nylons draped over chairs, assorted pieces of clothing tossed all around, and the bed itself unmade.

Seeing Marcia's expression, Evie shrugged and said, "The service is lousy in this place."

"You would think a house this big would have some kind of help," Marcia managed to say.

"There was a housekeeper and a handyman, but they left. Kind of at the last minute, you might say."

"But who will do the cooking for Mr. Spaniard? And, of course, for you and Mr. Janis?"

Evie placed her hands on her hips. "I'm no good in the kitchen. How about you?"

"My mother was a good cook and she was also a good teacher," Marcia said.

The tension between the two of them eased somewhat. "Good. You're hired. Now let's find something for you to wear."

Evie found a beige knit dress that looked as though it would fit Marcia. Then she fumbled in the depths of a closet and came up with a pair of brown pumps that were a perfect fit.

"Why don't you take the room across the hall?" Evie suggested. "I looked in there earlier and it's in good shape."

Marcia thanked her and walked across the hall to the opposite bedroom. Inside she found a comfortable canopied bed that had been made by some experienced hands. Probably the housekeeper before she left, Marcia thought.

The room was wallpapered in blue, with a silver pattern embossed on it. There was a braided oval rug on the floor that added a homey touch. And there were French doors that led to a balcony. Marcia sat down on a vanity bench and removed her shoes. Then she slipped out of her dress and into the one Evie had lent her. Looking in the mirror she saw that the dress was very becoming. At least Evie wasn't the flashy dresser that her fiance was.

A sudden gust of wind rattled the windows, reminding Marcia of the storm that still raged outside. She shivered as she watched the rain streak down the windows, remembering her experience of a half hour ago only too vividly. Idly she wondered if Joe had made it safely to shelter. No doubt he had. After all, he was employed here and should know his way around.

There was a sudden break in the wind, and in the silence that followed, Marcia thought she heard a tapping noise from the room next door. The sound came from the wall that separated the two rooms. Marcia walked across the room in the direction of the sound. But when she arrived at the wall, the tapping noise suddenly ceased. Then a fresh blast of wind struck the house and Marcia wondered if she had really heard the noise at all. Windcliff was rapidly becoming a house of mystery.

CHAPTER FOUR

There was a knock at the door and Marcia hurried to answer it. Brock Janis stood in the doorway.

"Very becoming," he said as his eyes swept over her dress. "I thought you might like a tour of the house. I got the impression this is your first visit to Windcliff."

"I'd like that very much," Marcia said, stepping quickly out of the room and shutting the door behind her. "And you're right. This is my first time on the island."

Somehow she had hoped it would be Evie who would take her on a tour of the house. She just didn't feel comfortable around Brock.

"As you already know, most of the bedrooms are on the second floor. There is another bedroom next to the library. It is currently being occupied by the man who brought you over from the mainland."

Marcia found it odd that one of the hired help would be sleeping in the main house.

"Of course, there is a small house on the island where the servants are boarded," Brock said.

Then Joe wasn't included in the class of servants. Just what role did he play in the household?

"This is Evie's room, as you have found out. I have the one next to her. There is nobody occupying the room adjacent to mine."

"Which is Mr. Spaniard's room?" Marcia asked.

"The admiral? He's in the end bedroom on your side of the house. It's the largest of the six upstairs rooms."

Marcia nodded her head. "Then Gregg Spaniard's room must be the one on the other side of mine. Am I correct?"

Brock's cold eyes seemed to bore an icy hole in her.

"You are. But as I've told you, Gregg is gone. Shall we go downstairs?"

As they went down the circular staircase, Marcia wondered about the noise she had heard in Gregg's room. For some reason she could not bring herself to mention what she had heard to Brock. After all, it could have been only her imagination, or the explanation might be quite a simple one. Many odd noises were heard in old houses. Since the sound had stopped, she did not see any reason to mention it to Brock.

"This is the dining room," Brock said needlessly as they walked into the long room not far from the end of the staircase.

The room had a long mahogany table that was flanked by what Marcia thought must be thirty chairs.

"The Spaniards must entertain a great deal," she said half to herself.

"I wouldn't know," Brock said. "The admiral and I have not corresponded much over the years. So I am almost as much a stranger here as you are."

Marcia had no way of disputing what Brock said. She had no way of disproving that he was not Gregg's cousin. All she had was a nagging suspicion that Brock Janis was not what he pretended to be.

At the rear of the dining room were windows that were streaked with the incessant downpouring of rain.

Marcia could see nothing beyond the windows but the gray, gloomy deluge of rain.

"Rain depresses me," Brock said, walking briskly to the windows and drawing the draperies.

"Did Joe make it back from the cove all right?" Marcia asked.

Brock nodded as he walked toward her. "He told me he lost sight of you, and when he went back to look, you had disappeared. He was quite worried about you."

Somehow Marcia found that hard to believe. Joe had shown no sign that he was concerned with her well-being from the time he had picked her up on the mainland until they reached the island.

"Come along, Marcia, there is still some of Windcliff you haven't seen."

Marcia allowed Brock to take her arm, but she kept a furtive eye out for Evie. Even though Brock was just being courteous, she was certain that Evie Andrews would take offense if she saw them together.

They walked through a wide, double-doored entrance off the right of the dining area into the adjacent study. So far this was the most comfortable room in the house. There were two wide French windows that on a more pleasant day would have given a splendid view of the grounds and possibly the open sea. Cozy, upholstered chairs were placed throughout the room and logs were set on the hearth. Brock set a match to them and soon they were crackling, giving off a friendly glow.

"Please sit down, Marcia," he said, indicating one of the chairs.

Fortunately, there was no couch in the room. Otherwise she felt certain Brock would have arranged it so that they sat on it together.

"Tell me about yourself. Have you always lived in Penwick?" he asked when he had settled himself in a chair opposite her.

"Yes. It's the only place I know. Oh, I've been to Portland and Bangor, but only on visits. Penwick's my home and it suits me fine."

"I see," Brock said, looking at her intently and tapping his fingertips together. "What of your family and friends? Do they all live in Penwick?"

"My parents are both dead. I'm an only child. And as far as my friends are concerned, they've all gone from Penwick."

Brock's cold eyes narrowed in a sardonic look. "Then you have nobody at Penwick who would be worried that you haven't returned from your mission? That you're spending the night here?"

Suddenly Marcia regretted that she had been so candid in her replies. Her mind raced to think of someone, anyone, with whom she could forge even the faintest tie.

"There is my neighbor, Clarita Hooper. I really should call her and let her know where I am. Would you mind if I used the telephone?"

Brock continued to stare at her and to tap his fingertips together. "There wouldn't be any point in trying to use the telephone. You see, the wires are dead. It must be the storm."

A hollow feeling of dread settled in Marcia's stomach. Here she was in a strange house on an unfamiliar island on a storm-tossed night, with no one to be concerned about her and no way to contact anyone even if there had been someone to care. She had never felt so totally alone and frightened in her entire life.

Across from her the flickering light from the flames

in the fireplace played coldly on Brock Janis's eyes. They were like the unblinking eyes of some fearsome reptile. She had to do something, make some movement to get away from their chilling stare.

"If you will show me where the kitchen is, I'll be glad to get dinner started," Marcia said.

Her words had the desired effect on Brock.

"Evie told me that you had volunteered your services. That was very thoughtful of you, Marcia. I must apologize for the lack of help. I am certain guests at Windcliff are not usually asked to work for their keep."

Marcia was on her feet and quick to assure Brock that she didn't in the least mind cooking. She did not dare tell him what was really on her mind, that she welcomed the task, anything to get as far away from him as possible.

From the study Brock led her back to the dining room and through a sliding door which opened onto the kitchen. It was not a large room like the others at Windcliff, but it was cheerful and Marcia felt that she was once again on familiar ground.

"The refrigerator is well stocked. Use whatever you wish," Brock said. "Would you like me to ask Evie to help?"

Marcia assured him that she could manage the job better alone. "You know the old saying: Too many cooks spoil the broth.'"

Brock shrugged and left the room.

Left alone Marcia heaved a big sigh of relief. Maybe she would have time to collect her thoughts now that she was alone.

She opened the refrigerator and found it was indeed well stocked. Marcia took out some pork chops which she decided she would bake. That with some green beans and a salad should be enough for the four of them.

As she busied herself in the kitchen, it was almost cozy, with the rain pattering against the windows. But she could not help feeling that something was wrong at Windcliff. Why had Gregg suddenly gone away to Boston? Why had the servants so unexpectedly left? Was Brock Janis really the person he said he was, or an imposter?

If Joe was employed by the Spaniards, why was he lodged in the main house and not in the servants' quarters? And who was in the room next to her upstairs? For now Marcia felt that she had not imagined the sound. Someone had been tapping on the walls as if he were trying to attract attention.

There was a telephone on the kitchen wall. Marcia picked it up to make certain that Brock had been telling the truth. The line was dead. She hung it up with a feeling of uneasiness. Once again she was reminded of the fact that there was no one outside of Clarita Hooper whom she could call if there was an emergency. Adam Long was somewhere in New York and he had not left a number where he could be reached.

Evie strolled into the kitchen as Marcia was taking the pork chops out of the oven.

"That smells good. I guess your mother did an all right job with you."

Marcia would have appreciated more help and less compliments. But Evie didn't offer any as she strolled out of the kitchen, leaving Marcia to set the table in the dining room, which seemed miles away from the kitchen. By the time the food was on the table, Marcia was inwardly fuming.

She was surprised when Joe joined them for supper.

The squat little man sat silently across from her, devouring his food noisily. Brock kept up a flow of conversation, but Marcia did not feel much like talking. Evie was indifferent to everything and only volunteered to speak when Brock spoke directly to her. Marcia had never felt more uncomfortable in her entire life.

As she poured coffee, Evie got to her feet. "Well, I guess I better take a tray up to the old man," she said and Marcia caught the quick look that was exchanged between Evie and Brock.

"Could I go with you? I'd like to see how Mr. Spaniard is doing," Marcia said.

After another exchange of glances between Brock and Evie, Evie said, "Why not? Only, it won't do any good. He can't speak, you know. He's completely paralyzed. Nothing but a vegetable."

Marcia winced at the matter-of-fact way Evie spoke of Joshia Spaniard. All the nurses she had come in contact with were generally sympathetic, although somewhat professional in their attitude toward their patients.

Evie fixed a tray and the two of them went upstairs. Passing the room next to hers, Marcia glanced at it wondering if someone was in there. And if so who it might be.

Evie didn't bother to knock but opened the door to Joshia's room and walked boldly inside. Somewhat timidly Marcia followed her. The room was vast with a high ceiling almost dwarfing the bed and its occupant. Even though there was a fire blazing on the hearth, there was a chill to the room.

When Marcia saw Joshia Spaniard, she almost gasped. This frail figure lying on the bed with snow-white hair and sunken eyes just couldn't be the

Joshia of her memories. As she neared the bed, his eyes fluttered open, the only visible sign of life in the emaciated body.

"Evening, admiral," Evie said. "How about some nice pork chops? We have a visitor. This is Marcia Carpenter from Penwick."

Evie put down the tray and said to Marcia, "He doesn't understand or feel anything. Paralyzed from the stroke. Can't move a muscle."

Joshia Spaniard's eyes were on Marcia, and for a moment she almost thought she saw a flicker of life in his eyes. Almost as though he were sending a message to her, a plea. Then the look vanished as Evie began to feed him.

Somewhere Marcia had read that even though the outward appearance of a stroke victim might indicate that he was not aware of what was happening around him, his brain was often still quite active. She resented the fact that Evie appeared to be so insensitive around the old man.

Marcia moved closer to the bed and as she did so Joshia's eyes shifted so they were upon her. As she stood there gazing into his eyes, they moved downward and back to her face. At first Marcia thought it had just been an involuntary movement. Then Joshia's eyes moved again. This time Marcia was sure it was not involuntary. She looked in the direction of Joshia's gaze and found herself staring at his hand that rested on the turned-down sheets. Slowly the index finger on Joshia's hand began to move.

CHAPTER FIVE

Marcia moved quickly toward the bed where Joshia lay. She was about to say something, to tell Evie that Joshia wasn't entirely motionless when she saw the look in his eyes. A warning look. It was almost as though she could read his thoughts, and he was telling her to say nothing to Evie. So Marcia held her tongue.

When Evie was finished, she picked up the tray and headed toward the door.

"Are you coming?" she said abruptly.

There was no way now that Marcia could remain in the room. Perhaps she could come back later when she could be alone with Joshia. She noticed that Evie did not lock the door when she shut it behind them.

It was early and Marcia was not tired, but she did not want to go back downstairs and spend the evening with Brock and Joe. So when she came to her room, she paused and said, "I think I'll turn in. I'm more tired than I thought I was."

"Yeah. Well, I guess you've had a rough day at that," Evie said as she headed down the hallway.

Marcia waited until she thought Evie had descended the staircase, then she hurried back to Joshia's room.

Evie had left a bedside lamp burning and its light fell upon the frail body lying on the bed. Marcia walked softly across the heavily carpeted floor thankful that her footsteps could not be heard below.

Joshia appeared to be sleeping. As Marcia stood by his bedside, his eyes opened and they seemed clear and lucid. At first Marcia was flustered, not knowing what to say. After all, she must have just appeared to be another stranger to Joshia.

Looking into those eyes that were still undimmed by time and every bit as bright as the ones in the portrait in the library, Marcia felt a smile tugging at the corners of her mouth.

"Mr. Spaniard, please excuse me. You don't know me, but I've seen you for many years in Penwick. My father was Cabot Carpenter. He was a fisherman. Perhaps you remember him."

Marcia did not know why she was saying all this to Joshia. Perhaps Evie was right and he could not understand what she was saying. But she had to try.

"I work for Adam Long. He asked me to bring some papers for Gregg's signature. That is why I am here."

Joshia's eyes were intent upon her. Not once while she spoke did they blink. It was such a peculiar feeling to be speaking to someone not knowing whether or not that person understood what you were saying.

"Gregg's cousin, Brock, has asked me to stay the night because of the storm."

At the mention of Brock, there was a sudden, radical change in Joshia's eyes. They darted from side to side in a frantic almost terrorized way.

"Mr. Spaniard, I've been told that you cannot move, but I saw you move the finger on your left hand. Do you think you can do it again?"

Joshia's eyes never left her face but Marcia's attention was all on Joshia's hand that lay inertly on the sheet of the bed. Slowly, almost imperceptibly, the index finger rose, then fell.

"That's wonderful!" Marcia exclaimed. "Then you really can hear me. Let's try a code. One lift of your finger for yes and two for no. Do you follow me, Mr. Spaniard?"

Slowly Joshia's finger rose once. Marcia almost shouted with joy. She would have to tell Brock what she had discovered. There was still hope for Joshia Spaniard.

"Brock will be pleased when I tell him that you can respond to questions," Marcia said.

There was a quick shifting of Joshia's eyes and Marcia saw his finger rise and lower, then rise once again.

"That was no. Don't you want me to tell Brock that you can hear and understand what's going on around you?"

Again Joshia signaled a negative response.

It would take forever asking questions to get the right answer from Joshia. So Marcia had to think of some other way to question him.

On the nightstand next to his bed was a small tablet and a pencil. Marcia reached for these and said, "I'll go through the alphabet. When I come to a letter that will spell a word you signal me with yes."

Slowly Marcia started at the beginning of the alphabet. She paused after each letter to give Joshia time to communicate with her. When she got to d, there was a response. Marcia wrote the first letter of the word on the blank sheet of paper. This was a good beginning. Starting all over again she wrote the next letter of the alphabet at Joshia's signal.

After the fifth letter was written, Marcia was becoming uneasy. The incompleted word stared at her from the whiteness of the paper. If she was correct, only one more letter remained to complete the word.

Slowly she went through the alphabet once more. Finally, Joshia's finger moved. Now she knew that what she had feared was a reality. She stared at the word that the old man had painstakingly spelled out to her. DANGER!

She could feel a cold chill touch the nape of her neck. The only sound in the room was the splattering of rain as gusts of wind struck the windows.

In a hoarse, half whisper, Marcia asked, "Danger? Danger from what?"

But Joshia's eyelids flickered as he fell asleep. This had been very taxing for the old man. He was still a very sick person and even this small exertion of energy had taken its toll. Marcia quietly tore the piece of paper from the pad and stuffed it into a pocket of her dress. Then she went swiftly out of the room. It was all she could do to stem the impulse to run down the hall to her room. Suddenly the walls of Windcliff seemed to be reaching out to her with haunted, clutching hands. There was no escaping their malignancy. When she got to her room, she quickly shut the door behind her and tried to lock it, but the door could only be locked from the outside.

Marcia pulled a chair from across the room and wedged it under the knob. At least now she would have some warning if someone tried to come into her room.

She sat by the window and watched the angry torrent of rain batter the panes. Here she was in Windcliff, the house of her dreams, only to find that the dream had suddenly become a nightmare. Where was Gregg? Had he really gone away so unexpectedly to Boston? What danger had Joshia tried to warn her against? Was it danger from a person?

There was no way that she could telephone for help. If only Adam Long hadn't gone to New York on business. Even if he hadn't, she could not reach him and find out if Gregg really had a cousin named Brock Janis. She suddenly felt trapped, a prisoner in this big, gloomy house in the middle of the bay.

She wondered who might be in the room next door. It was wildly improbable, but it just might be Gregg in there. Maybe he hadn't gone away, after all. Perhaps he might be in his room, bound and gagged or injured in some way.

"Hold on, girl," Marcia said aloud. "You're letting your imagination run away with you. It's the storm that's getting to you."

Deciding that that must be the reason for her nervousness Marcia felt somewhat better. After all, she might never see Windcliff again. From the inside, that is. Tomorrow the storm would be gone and she would be back on the mainland. All of the mystery of the house would disappear with the morning light.

Still, Joshia had spelled out danger. But maybe it had just been an accident. Perhaps there was another word he had wanted to say and had somehow gotten the spelling mixed up in his head.

Looking around the room, she found a book in the top drawer of the dresser. It was a classic by Charles Dickens, not the sort of thing she was in the mood for. But at least it would be something to while away the time until she became sleepy enough to go to bed.

A half hour had passed and she heard someone in the hall near her room. Marcia hurriedly removed the chair, switched off the light, and carefully opened the door. In the shadowy hallway she saw Brock Janis as he went into the room next door. Marcia quickly shut the door, braced the chair against it, and snapped on the light. She listened intently and above the roaring of the wind she thought she heard voices from next door. It was impossible to tell through the wall and over the keening wind whom Brock was talking to. It might have been either Evie or Joe. Then there was silence next door. Marcia stood with her heart pounding for what seemed an eternity. Then the door to the room next to her was opened and closed once more.

Marcia waited until she heard the footsteps go away again. Whoever Brock had been talking to had not come out of the room with him. Was Joe or Evie still in the room? And if so, for what purpose? Marcia glanced at her watch. It was only eight o'clock. Suddenly she got the feeling that she had forgotten something. She paced the floor trying to remember what it was. Then in a quick flash she remembered. She had left the documents in the library.

It took all the courage she could summon to remove the chair from against the door, but she had been entrusted with the papers by Adam. She had to get them from the library, regardless of whom she might meet in doing so.

The hall outside her room was brightly lighted, but when she reached the staircase, she found herself in shadows. Joshia's message pounded in her ears as she began to descend the circular staircase. Danger! Danger! The rain had slackened, but the wind still howled around the eaves and corners of the old building.

When she reached the landing of the staircase, Marcia paused. She heard voices in what sounded like a heated argument. Across from her the door was open slightly to Joe's room. She heard Brock's voice rising angrily.

"You should have gotten rid of her like I told you.

We can't have her snooping around here. Why didn't you do what I told you?"

Joe's answer was muffled. It was Evie's voice she heard next. "Lay off him, Brock. He did the best he could. Anyway, we can keep an eye on her. Make sure she doesn't see anything she shouldn't."

Marcia's hands turned to ice. Were they talking about her? The Brock she heard speaking now was not the smooth, suave Brock who had met her at the door only hours before. There was a toughness in his voice, a cruelty that frightened her.

Now she had to get the documents for certain. She had no idea who Brock Janis was and what he and the others were doing at Windcliff. The only thing she was certain of was that he could not be Gregg's cousin.

With quick steps Marcia hurried across the wide hall being careful not to make any sound that would attract the three in Joe's room.

Inside the library she found the folder with the documents where she had left them. Thank heavens Brock hadn't noticed her putting them beside the chair. With nervous, trembling hands, Marcia grabbed the folder and hurried out of the room.

Directly across from her the door to the study stood open. If she went through the study, she could then go into the dining room and slip up the staircase. There would be less chance of her being seen that way. Marcia felt she would be safer if Brock and the others did not know that she had overheard their conversation. Marcia made her way to the study where, fortunately, someone had left a light burning. She entered the dining room, then suddenly felt thirsty.

So she went to the kitchen. There she happened to notice that the dishes from the night's dinner had been haphazardly stacked. But what caught her attention were the two trays that lay on the drainboard. Two! Someone besides Joshia had had his food taken to him this evening. It must have been Brock who had brought the second tray to whoever occupied the room next to her.

Marcia quickly took a drink, then went back to the dining room. As she moved cautiously to reach the staircase and then the safety of her room, she could not help but wonder who the person was in the room next to her own. It hadn't been Joe or Evie whom Brock had spoken to when he entered the room. Someone was either sick or being held captive in that room. Could it be Gregg? But he had gone to Boston. Or had he? She had only Brock's word for that.

Maybe it was the nurse who really hadn't left the house, after all. Or it could be some person whose identity Marcia didn't even know.

Coming out of the dining room, she slackened her pace. She paused by the doorway and listened. The voices were still engaged in a heated conversation. Just as she was about to emerge from the dining room, Brock walked out of Joe's room. Marcia quickly stepped back into the shadows. Her breath caught in her throat because she was not certain that she hadn't been seen. From where she stood in the shadows she could see and not be seen. Brock stood for a moment looking at the staircase. Even in the dim light of the hall she could see hard lines on his face.

It seemed an eternity before he pivoted and returned to Joe's bedroom. Seizing that moment Marcia rushed quickly up the staircase and didn't stop until she had reached the top. She hurried down the short, darkened hallway to the main hall. But she did not go immediately to her room. Instead she tiptoed to the door for fear that her actions might be heard downstairs. A sudden gust of wind struck the house, rattling the shutters on the windows at the end of the hall. This sent her scurrying to her room.

Inside, Marcia once again braced the door with the chair for whatever safety that might offer her. She did not feel at all secure in this house anymore. She shed her dress and went to bed in her slip. Somehow she felt more secure with the heavy spread pulled up to her chin. She left the lamp burning on the nightstand to ward off the deadly shadows of Windcliff. The house was quiet except for the sound of the ever-present wind as it battered the walls.

CHAPTER SIX

For Marcia it was one of the longest nights of her life. She tossed and turned and finally drifted off to sleep from sheer exhaustion. Her dreams were troubled, and when she awoke she felt as though she hadn't slept a wink.

Thank heavens the storm was over. Bright sunlight filtered through the windows making a filigree pattern on the bedspread. Marcia got out of bed and washed her face with cold water. This revived her and seemed to freshen her low spirits.

The dress that she had worn crossing the bay yesterday was dry, and she slipped it on. It felt good to be wearing her own things once again. She took her comb out of her purse and ran it through her short brown hair. Then she put a faint gloss to her lips.

She walked to the French doors and opened them, admiring her little balcony. Stepping out into the crisp morning air, she took a deep breath. In the distance, she could see the mainland clearly. As she stood there, a feeling came over her. A feeling that eyes were watching her. Marcia looked down from the balcony on short, stunted bushes and the grounds of Windcliff which led to the rocky cliffs. The sea was an expanse of blue with milky whitecaps stirred up by the restless tide. She could not shake off the feeling that she was being watched.

Turning to the left, she saw where her balcony ended and another began a short distance away, outside the adjacent room. In the other direction was a third balcony, so that each bedroom was provided with its own balcony.

The house did not seem so forbidding in the clear light of day. After breakfast she no doubt would be returning to the mainland. Now that the storm was past, there would be no reason for her to remain at Windcliff. As she stood there, the memory of the conversation she had overheard last night flooded her mind.

What if she was not allowed to return to Penwick? What if Brock wanted her to remain on the island? But that was impossible. There wasn't any reason for her to stay. She had seen nothing. She knew nothing that would incriminate the three.

Then she thought about Joshia. Hadn't she learned that he was able to hear what went on around him? Yet only she knew this. There was no way that Brock or Evie could have uncovered what she knew. When she returned to Penwick she would make inquiries about the nurse and if she found Joshia's doctor, she'd tell him what she had learned of the old man.

With this resolution Marcia went back into her room, removed the chair from the door, and stepped into the hall. Evie was just coming out of her own room. She was dressed in rust-colored slacks with a red silk blouse that clashed disturbingly with her orange hair. Her makeup was even heavier this morning, as though she were trying to disguise her lack of sleep.

"Good morning," Marcia said cheerily.

Evie shot her a glacial look. "What's good about it? I didn't sleep a wink last night. That howling wind gave me the heebie-jeebies."

Marcia did not reply. She did not want Evie to know that she hadn't slept any better for fear that Evie might wonder why.

"You'll feel better after a cup of coffee," Marcia said, heading for the staircase. "Are you coming?"

"In a minute. I have to get Brock up."

Evie yawned and ran her fingers through the mop of orange hair as she moved listlessly toward Brock's room.

The stairway was not the creepy frightening place it had been last night. Marcia hurried down its twisting length, stopping at the landing as the door to Joe's room was flung open.

Joe stood there wearing grease-stained pants and a faded, wrinkled shirt. His beady eyes glared at her from beneath his heavy brows. Marcia felt herself angered by his insolent look.

"You fixin' breakfast?" he said in a croaking voice.

Marcia nodded.

"I like my eggs sunny side up."

"You'll take them scrambled or go without," Marcia found herself saying. She would not be intimidated by this disagreeable man.

Joe gave her a final glowering look, then retreated to his room.

Marcia stalked across the hall, her good mood shattered by her encounter with Joe. She flung open the kitchen door and went inside.

Opening the refrigerator, she took out some sausages and a carton of eggs. As she set them down, she glanced at where the two trays had been last night. They were gone. She quickly opened the cabinet doors and in one cabinet found the trays neatly washed and stacked. Evie must have been here before she went to bed last night.

Marcia's angry mood was replaced by a quiet, creeping dread. They were making certain that their tracks were well covered. If Marcia had discovered the two trays, there might have been questions to be answered. Silently Marcia prayed that this nightmare would be over, that she would return to Penwick safe and unharmed.

She busied herself in preparing breakfast to keep her mind occupied. When she had set the table in the dining room, Evie and Brock walked in, followed by a disgruntled Joe.

"Well, what a pleasant surprise, Marcia," Brock said.

Evie glared at Brock. "Are you referring to the table or the help?" she said with a twist to her lips.

"To both, my dear," Brock said, pulling out a chair for Evie, which temporarily placated her.

"I'll bring you some coffee," Marcia said, retreating from the room. She did not want a scene this morning. If anything, she did not want any disagreement. Otherwise her departure might be delayed.

She poured coffee, being careful not to overlook Joe. After all, he would be the one to take her back to Penwick.

"Did you sleep well, Marcia?" Brock asked, taking a sip of coffee.

"Very well. It was a very comfortable bed," Marcia said as she headed for the kitchen once more to bring in the sausages, eggs, and toast.

Everyone seemed to have a good appetite. Everyone but Marcia. Her stomach was in knots of anticipation. She moved the food around on her plate to give the impression that she was eating. Joe devoured his food with his usual noisy gusto. Brock and Evie did not appear to notice his uncouth table manners.

As they were all sipping a second cup of coffee, Brock said, "It would appear that our storm is over. And none too soon for me."

"You can say that again," Evie said with an undisguised shudder. "As far as I am concerned, Teal Island is for the birds. The sooner we get out of here, the better."

Marcia pretended that she hadn't heard that remark or seen the looks exchanged by Evie and Brock.

"How soon do you think I'll be able to return to Penwick?" Marcia asked, trying to sound as casual as possible.

"Can't go back. Not till I get that boat fixed," Joe said, devouring a slice of toast.

"What do you mean? What's the matter with the boat?" Marcia asked, her worst fears slowly being realized.

"Storm damaged the boat," Joe said and his beady eyes looked mockingly at her.

"How soon will it be fixed? I have to get back to my job," Marcia said, her hands clutching the arms of her chair.

"Perhaps Mr. Long will send a boat for you," Brock said evenly.

"He's not there. He had to go to New York on business," Marcia blurted out and then could have bitten her tongue.

A crafty smile spread across Brock's pale features. "Then there really isn't any need for you to hurry back to your work. As long as your boss is gone, you might as well enjoy your stay. Give yourself a vacation."

Evie stirred impatiently in her chair. Marcia could see that the thought of her remaining another night under the same roof was as unpleasant to Evie as it was to herself.

"Don't just sit there, Joe. Get a move on. Fix that boat," Evie said.

"I take my orders from Brock," Joe said, ignoring Evie. "And from Brock alone."

"You can be replaced," Evie said with an arching eyebrow.

Joe did nothing to disguise his anger. "That goes for you too, Miss High and Mighty."

Suddenly Evie and Joe were going at it tooth and nail. It was Brock who broke them up. "That will do. We have a guest. Now, Joe, I suggest you see what can be done about the boat."

Joe got to his feet, almost knocking his chair over backward. "Okay. But you tell Evie to keep her yap shut. Or there's going to be trouble."

With that Joe stomped out of the room. Evie had a gloating look on her face as though she had won that round.

What have I gotten myself into? Marcia thought. Who are these people, and what are they doing in Gregg's house? If only he would return this morning.

"You must excuse Joe, Marcia. He has a short fuse," Brock said.

"If everyone is finished, I'll clean up the dishes," Marcia said.

"Need any help?" Evie asked unenthusiastically.

"No thanks. I work better alone," Marcia said, tempted to overturn Evie's cup of coffee onto her lap.

"Whatever," Evie said. "I'll go upstairs and take the admiral a tray."

"And I have work to do in the library," Brock said, getting to his feet.

Evie didn't say a word to Marcia as she fixed Joshia's breakfast. But as she started out the door, she said, "Just because Brock says you're welcome here, that doesn't go for everybody."

Before Marcia could think of a quick retort, Evie had left the kitchen. She didn't cotton to staying at Windcliff any more than Evie wanted her to. Maybe Joe would get the boat repaired and she could be off the island by noon.

He seemed to obey any order that Brock gave him. It was such a weird relationship. Joe certainly was not one of the regular hired help at Teal Island. He must have come along with Brock and Evie. It just didn't make sense. If Brock had only come to visit Joshia, why did he bring his own help with him? Marcia felt that there was more to their relationship than met the eye.

It was obvious that there was no love lost between Joe and Evie. Also, the way the two had acted at breakfast had dispelled any thoughts of Joe being a servant.

When Marcia had finished the dishes, she decided to go for a walk. Anything to get out of the gloomy atmosphere of the house. She opened a door but found that it led to the cellar rather than the outdoors. A long narrow flight of stairs went down to the murky depths of the cellar.

Marcia shivered and was about to close the door when she saw a small plastic packet lying on the top step. She reached down and picked it up. It contained a white grainy substance. Either salt or sugar, she figured and then absently tucked the small bag into a pocket of her dress. The cook must have dropped it there and forgotten about it.

She closed the door to the cellar with a faint shudder and tried a second door which, to her relief, led her to the outside.

The sky was a bright periwinkle blue with a scattering of a few fleecy clouds. It was good to be outside the walls of Windcliff. Marcia followed a flagstone walk that was bordered with well-trimmed shrubbery. It was evident that someone had been taking care of the grounds on Teal Island and quite recently.

The path she was following took her behind the house and into a garden. Here Marcia found a profusion of flowers growing in the rock soil. She paused and, glancing back at the mansion, thought she saw a quick movement at a window, as though a curtain had been hastily dropped. Someone had been watching her from the window. It was either Evie or Brock. Joe had gone to see about the boat. Her actions would be observed wherever she went on the island. Even with the curtain drawn over the window she still felt that she was being watched. Only, whoever was watching her was not in the house.

Uneasily Marcia followed the path that meandered out of the garden. The path wound its way to the edge of a high cliff. Below her the turbulent sea crashed with a deafening roar against the shoals and rocks in the bay. It would be suicidal for anyone to attempt to swim in that swirling, churning water.

Marcia cast one fleeting, hopeless look at Penwick across the bay wondering when, if ever, she would see her home again. Here, on the high sweep of the cliff, she felt the watcher's eyes more strongly upon her. Where was the watcher? Who was keeping such close tabs on her movements?

With a nervous sigh she turned and continued her walk along the flagstone path. Ahead of her, where the path ended, stood a small cottage. It must be the servants' quarters, she reckoned as she quickened her step.

When she arrived at the small house, she saw that all the windows were barred with wooden storm windows. Joe must have secured them because of last night's storm.

The path terminated at the door to the cottage, but when Marcia tried the door she found that it was locked. Slowly Marcia walked around the building to see if there might be another entrance on the windward side. As she stepped around the corner of the building, a gust of wind struck her. There was little protection on this side of the house from the ever-present wind, and in the distance she could see the ocean stretching toward the horizon.

To her dismay she found that the other door to the house was also locked. Joe had done a thorough job of securing the building. She hurried around the structure to get away from the force of the wind and found herself once more near the front door.

As she started to move past the front door, something attracted her attention. Something caught in a clump of shrubbery that bracketed the front of the house.

Marcia reached down and picked up a white object—a nurse's cap! What was a cap doing here, so far from the house? Had the nurse lost it somehow, and had it blown away, becoming entangled in the brush by the servants' quarters? It was possible. But somehow Marcia did not believe that. What she did believe was that the answer to how the cap got there lay inside the little cottage.

She was so wrapped up in her thoughts and in the small white cap that she did not see the person who approached until a shadow fell across her.

CHAPTER SEVEN

"I'll take that," came Joe's voice as he gruffly snatched the cap out of her hand.

Marcia instinctively cringed as Joe reached out and grabbed her by the arm.

"Your snoopin' has gotten you into trouble this time, miss. Come on, we're going to see Brock."

Marcia winced under the pressure of Joe's hand as he forced her to walk up the pathway that led to Windcliff. Joe was silent as they trudged along and Marcia found that it was useless to try to escape from his painful grasp. The experience was both hurtful and humiliating to her.

When they arrived at the kitchen door, Joe flung it open and thrust her inside. Without waiting for her to say anything, he again grabbed her arm and ushered her into the library.

"What's going on here?" Brock said, slamming shut the drawer in the desk where he had been sitting.

"I found her prowling around down by the servants' quarters," Joe said.

"Miss Carpenter is not a prisoner, Joe. She can come and go as she pleases," Brock said with an apologetic smile.

"That ain't all. She found this when she was nosing around down there." Joe brandished the nurse's cap and Brock's smile crumbled on his lips.

"That's was unfortunate." Brock's face became hard as granite. "I see that you have had too much freedom at Windcliff. Now I see that we have been too generous."

Marcia found her voice. "I don't know what you're talking about. And I certainly don't appreciate being manhandled by Joe. How soon may I leave the island?"

Brock glanced at Joe, then down at Marcia. "The boat hasn't been repaired yet. Unfortunately, your departure will be delayed. But while you are with us, certain precautionary measures will be taken."

"What are you hinting at?" Marcia said with a bravado she did not feel.

"I am not hinting at anything. Joe is going to take you to your room where you will be locked in."

Marcia started to protest.

"For your own protection," said Brock and he dismissed them with a nod of his head.

Joe reached for her arm, but she flung his hand away.

"That won't be necessary. I'll go peacefully."

Marcia walked out of the room with Joe at her side. She thought about breaking into a run, but where could she run to? Joe knew the island better than she and there was no way to reach the mainland except by boat. Swimming was out of the question.

This all seemed like a horrible nightmare. As though it were all happening to somebody else. What had she stumbled onto in coming to Teal Island? Brock thought that she had unearthed some secret when she had found the nurse's cap. How little he knew. As far as Marcia was concerned, she was as much in the dark as she had been last night when she arrived at Windcliff.

As they arrived at the staircase, Evie was coming down. She was carrying two trays, and when she saw Marcia, she put them together in a vain attempt to disguise the second one.

"Where are you two going in such an all-fired hurry?" Evie asked, trying to divert Marcia's attention from the trays.

"If it's any of your business, Brock wants me to lock the little lady in her room. Seems she has a bad case of snoopitis."

There was almost a look of glee on Evie's face and she switched the trays so that she was carrying one in each hand. It was almost as though she were saying, "What difference does it make now?"

"Too bad, Marcia," she said aloud. "But you've got a nice comfortable room. Make the most of it."

Joe made a motion to reach for Marcia's arm, but she started up the stairs with as much bravery as she could muster.

"Brock still in the library?" Evie asked.

"See for yourself," Joe snarled and Evie stomped angrily across the wide hall.

When they reached Marcia's room, Joe opened the door and stood outside until she walked in. Then he slammed the door behind her. Marcia heard the unmistakable clicking of a key in the lock. Instinctively she tried the doorknob. It turned under the pressure of her hand, but the lock beneath it held the door securely in place.

It took Marcia a few minutes to realize that she was now a prisoner at Windcliff. Only a few hours earlier she had arisen with the hope that she would be back at Penwick shortly after breakfast. Now she was locked in her room. And she had no idea why.

Marcia paced the room, mentally going over what

had happened since her arrival that would have placed her in such jeopardy. Had it been the fact that she had gone to see Joshia alone? Perhaps someone had seen her go into his room and had figured that she had stumbled onto something. Perhaps, after all, Brock and Evie did know that Joshia was able to hear and respond in his feeble way.

That might have been the reason, but she doubted it. If anything, it had something to do with her finding the nurse's cap.

Marcia sat down on the bed. Pacing would not do her any good. And she thought better when she was sitting down.

If Brock had been angered over her finding the nurse's cap, then something must have happened to the person wearing it. He had not been disturbed until Joe had mentioned that cap, and then he had changed.

Then there was Evie and the two trays. Someone was definitely in the next room. Someone who had tapped on the wall last night. Was that person a prisoner like herself?

Perhaps it was the nurse. Yes, that could very well be. It would certainly tie in with the missing cap. But Brock had said she had gone to the mainland with Gregg. Had that just been a story he had concocted to make up for the nurse's absence?

The more Marcia thought about Brock, Evie, and Joe, the more she was convinced that they had nothing to do with the Spaniards. But what were they doing on Teal Island? It was evident that they were up to no good.

If the boat hadn't been damaged by the storm, she might have been out of here, away from this troubled house. Surely there had to be more than one boat on the island. The Spaniards were wealthy enough to have a fleet of boats.

Then it became clear to Marcia that the story of the damaged boat was just that. A story. They had no intention of letting her leave the island. How long, she wondered, did they intend keeping her a prisoner in this room?

Marcia sat on the bed for hours, all kinds of thoughts tumbling over and over in her mind. She was startled when she heard a key being turned in the lock and saw the door open.

It was Evie.

"Here's your lunch," she said, putting a plate down on a chair. On the plate was a tuna-fish sandwich. "Like I told you, I'm no cook."

Marcia glared at Evie. "I'm not hungry."

Evie shrugged. "Suit yourself. I'll leave the sandwich. If you get hungry enough, you'll eat it."

Marcia decided to try another approach. "Evie, I'm sorry. Can't we be friends? Could you stay and talk a little while?"

Evie was wary, but she did not leave.

"What's there to talk about?"

"I was wondering. How long have you known Brock?"

At the mention of Brock's name, Evie's face lost its hardness. "That's an easy one. A year ago last month. We met in Miami. A friend of mine introduced us. We went out a few times and that was all I needed."

"Are you really engaged?" Marcia asked, trying to keep Evie talking.

"In a way. No ring or nothing like that. After we leave this place, Brock promised we'd get married. Nothing fancy. Justice of the peace. But that's all right with me. I just want to be Mrs. Brock Janis."

"Do you think it will happen?"

Evie stiffened. "Of course, it will. Brock promised that if I went along with him, we'd get married."

"Why did you come to Windcliff? Was it to get Joshia's approval?"

"That's a laugh. Brock doesn't care about the admiral. He's got other things on his mind. Teal Island just happened to be the handiest place."

Marcia couldn't stop now. "Then Brock really didn't come here to see his Cousin Gregg."

"His cousin! Brock never heard of the Spaniards until a day before we got here."

Although Marcia had been suspecting as much, the words that Evie spoke still came as a shock to her. "Then Brock isn't Gregg's cousin?"

Evie walked to the door. When she turned to face Marcia, the hard lines had once again returned to her face. "You ask too many questions."

With that, Evie walked out of the room, slamming and locking the door behind her. Marcia was once more a prisoner.

Now that she was once again alone, Marcia looked at the unappetizing sandwich. She picked it up and took a bite. Evie was right. She couldn't cook.

The room, which had been so pleasant before, now seemed to close in on Marcia. She had no idea how long she would be forced to stay here. She could only think about getting out and trying to escape from the island. Yet Marcia knew that even if she succeeded in fleeing from the house, there was still the water of the bay to contend with. There was no way that she could swim to the mainland. Her fear of the cold dark water came back to haunt her.

Marcia walked over to the French doors that opened onto the balcony. She pushed them open and stepped cautiously out. When she neared the railing of the balcony, she looked down. It was quite a distance to the ground. There was no trellis or ladder or anything she could use to lower herself to the earth below. If she jumped, it would mean a broken leg or even possibly a concussion. It all seemed so hopeless. She stepped back when she saw the shadow of a man below the balcony. As she stood there, Joe ambled across the lawn muttering to himself. Marcia slipped behind the protection of one of the open doors just as Joe paused and glanced in her direction.

From where she stood she could follow his movements without being seen. Joe was heading purposefully in the direction of the cliffs.

He was headed toward a building whose roof Marcia could see from where she stood. Maybe this was the boathouse that held the Spaniard boats. It was a perfect location for one, nestled between two high cliffs which offered a natural harbor.

For a moment there was a fleeting ray of hope in Marcia's heart. If she could somehow make it down the walls of Windcliff she might have a chance to see what was in the boathouse. Then she sighed. What good would that do? Even if there were a hundred boats down there, she didn't know how to operate one. Everything was hopeless.

She watched dejectedly as Joe disappeared down the trail as it dipped below her vision. Then she turned to go inside. As she did, she saw the two balconies that were parallel to hers. One of them, she knew, belonged to Joshia's room. The other one must belong to Gregg's room. But Gregg was away. Now there was someone else in that room. Marcia felt that it might possibly be the nurse who had been attending to Joshia. Who else could it be? Since the cap she found had upset Brock, she assumed his reaction was due to the fact that the nurse had not left the island, after all.

Marcia moved to the end of her balcony. Even

though the next balcony was quite close, she could not step from her own onto it. If she could find something to use as a plank, she could easily gain access to the other balcony. Once there, she might be able to find out who was in that mysterious room.

Hurrying back into her own room, she reached frantically for something to use to bridge the gap between the two balconies. She opened the dresser drawer and removed one of the drawers. Then she hurried back to the balcony but found the drawer fell just a few inches short of closing the gap. Frustrated, Marcia returned to the room.

She checked the closets, then looked beneath the bed. She even thought of using a chair but abandoned that idea. Finally with an exasperated sigh, she returned to the balcony. It was so near and yet all she could do was stand there and stare at the other balcony.

"It's so close, a frog could leap over to it," Marcia muttered to herself. Then a thought crossed her mind. If she stood on the railing of her balcony, she could easily jump to the next one. It might be a little risky, but then she was in a desperate situation.

Kicking off her shoes, Marcia grabbed the supporting column and stepped onto the flat surface of the railing. She teetered there for a moment, not daring to look down for fear of losing her nerve. Then, taking a deep breath, she leaped across the short distance and landed on the floor of the next balcony. In the event she had to return hastily to her room, she knew that she could do it without any great effort.

Now that she was on the next balcony, Marcia found that there were French doors like those leading to her room. She moved quietly to the doors and tried to look inside, but the drapes were drawn and she could see nothing. As she reached for the doorknob, she heard the sound of footsteps below and Marcia cowered against the closed doors. Her heart was pounding so furiously that she could feel its pulsation in her ears.

Below her, through the ornately carved grillework of the balcony railing, she saw the unmistakable blond hair of Brock Janis. She silently prayed that he would not look up to where she stood. Her prayers were answered and, without an upward glance, Brock returned to the house.

Marcia felt her knees begin to quaver from her near brush with discovery. She leaned against the doors until the feeling passed. Now that she felt more steady she once again reached for that doorknob.

Slowly the doorknob turned beneath her grasp. It opened without a sound and Marcia stepped quickly into the darkened room. She stood there for a few moments until her eyes became accustomed to the faint gloom. There was not a sound in the room except her own light breathing, but she had the feeling that she was not alone.

Then she saw a person slumped in a chair, bound and gagged. As she stood there, the person slowly looked in her direction. It was Gregg Spaniard.

CHAPTER EIGHT

Marcia stared unbelievingly at Gregg. Even in the dim light of the room, his handsome dark features were outstanding. Then he made a motion with his head toward the ropes that bound him to the chair. Marcia recovered her senses and rushed to his aid.

She loosened the gag from his mouth, and he took a deep gulp of air.

"You've got to be a guardian angel," he said, looking at her with his dark eyes, which up close were flecked with gold.

"I'm afraid not. I'm Marcia Carpenter. How did you get into this mess?" she said, attacking the ropes that bound his body.

"It's a long story. I'll tell you when I get some circulation back in my arms."

Marcia had untied the knots of the rope behind the chair and Gregg's arms were free. He rubbed them for a few minutes, then quickly freed himself from the rest of the ropes.

As he massaged his legs, he looked at her and said, "I know who you are. You were with Adam Long the other night. Only, that wasn't the first time I've seen you. You grew up in Penwick, didn't you?"

Marcia was surprised that Gregg had even noticed her. He had never given the impression that he had given her a second thought.

"Yes. I lived with my parents before they both died. Then, after school, I got a job in Adam Long's legal office."

Gregg's eyes never left her face. He was one of those people who gave their complete attention to whomever was talking to them. It was a trait that Marcia always liked in a person. Adam Long always seemed to be preoccupied with either making an impression or only interested in your response to his conversation.

"Are you all right?" Marcia asked as Gregg got unsteadily to his feet.

"A little wobbly, but I'll be fine," Gregg said as he leaned against the chair for support.

"Was it your cousin who did this?" Marcia asked in an effort to get Gregg to talk.

"My cousin?" Gregg asked, surprised.

"Brock Janis. He told me he was your cousin. He said something about you being called away to Boston on some urgent matter. You weren't expected back until today or even later."

A wry smile tugged at Gregg's lips. "I've never seen the man before. I have a cousin, but he lives in Australia. Brock and his henchman and that girl broke into the house two nights ago. He forced me into this room and tied me up."

Looking at Gregg's tall, muscular physique, it was hard for Marcia to realize what he was saying was true. It must have shown in her face.

"He had a gun. Otherwise he wouldn't have gotten away with it. Then they threatened to harm my father if I didn't cooperate."

Marcia wouldn't put it past Brock to hold that kind of threat over Gregg's head.

"But why are they here? What do they want?" Marcia asked urgently.

Gregg shook his head. "I wish I knew. It all happened so quickly. Before I realized it, I was up in my room, bound and gagged. When I tried to question Brock, he put this gag in my mouth. I'm worried sick about my dad. If they've harmed him…"

Marcia quickly set his mind at rest. "Your father is fine. I saw him yesterday. Evie brings him food and sees that he eats."

Gregg ran a hand through his dark, wavy hair. "I suppose I should be thankful for that. Only, it burns me up that they can just walk into a house and take over. You don't know how it feels to be a prisoner in your own home."

Marcia was about to answer that when Gregg said, "I'm sorry. I shouldn't be unburdening myself to you like this."

"I don't mind," Marcia said. "Considering we're both in the same boat, so to speak."

"You mean they locked you in your room, too?"

Marcia nodded.

"Why? What did you do?" Gregg asked, his dark eyes intent on her.

"Search me. All I know is that when I went for a walk this morning, I happened to find a nurse's cap. That seemed to infuriate Brock and he had me locked in my room."

"Then they've probably done something to Nurse Daniels. She was supposed to leave and see about a replacement." Gregg shook his head, then said, "If they locked you in your room, how did you manage to get here?"

"Like your room, they didn't bother with the French doors. I went out on the balcony and managed to leap from my balcony to yours."

"You're quite a person. Thank you, Marcia

Carpenter," Gregg said, and Marcia felt her face redden.

"Mr. Spaniard, do you think Brock and Evie and Joe are dangerous?"

Gregg reached out and took one of Marcia's hands in his. "Please call me Gregg."

"Very well, Gregg. If you'll call me Marcia."

"Marcia it is."

"Your father told me there was danger here."

Gregg's reaction was immediate. "Dad spoke to you?"

"Not verbally. We worked out a system. I went through the alphabet and when I came to a letter that meant something to him, he would raise a finger. It took a long time, but the word he spelled out was danger. Then he fell asleep."

"He was trying to warn you. To probably leave the island."

"I couldn't do that. Brock said the boat was damaged during the storm. Joe was supposed to be repairing it when he caught me near that small cottage."

"The servants' quarters. I wonder how Carl and Maggie are doing."

"Carl and Maggie? Who are they?" Marcia asked at the mention of two unfamiliar names.

"They're the Holts. A married couple. Carl is the gardener and handyman and Maggie runs the house."

At the mention of the Holts, Marcia knew who Gregg was referring to. She had seen them many times at Penwick and knew they worked at Windcliff. She had never heard them referred to by their first names before.

"I haven't seen them anywhere around the house," Marcia said. "Evie said they had left unexpectedly."

"Then Brock and his gang have done something with them also. If I only knew what they were up to."

"You don't think they are thieves, do you? It's possible they plan on looting the house. But with their boat damaged, they'll have to wait to haul everything away."

Gregg shook his head.

"No, they're not thieves. There are three serviceable crafts in the boathouse. If they had planned on stealing anything, they could easily take one of the boats."

"Then whatever reason could they be here for?"

"I wish I knew. But one thing is certain—they know all about Teal Island. They knew that Dad was sick and where the boathouse was and the servants' quarters. I think they checked out the island before they made their move."

Marcia sat down on a plush, high-backed chair. Gregg remained standing, grateful to be released from the ropes that had bound him.

"I'm sorry you got involved in all this," Gregg finally said. "You're just an innocent bystander."

"Not anymore, I'm afraid. Brock seemed to feel that I know more than I'm letting on. I guess I wouldn't have been suspicious at all if I hadn't heard you tapping on the wall last night."

Gregg's dark eyes became thoughtful. "Then you did hear me? I thought it might be you in the next room."

"At first I couldn't be sure I heard anything. I went to the wall to listen, but with the thunder and rain I didn't hear anything."

"That must have been when Brock came into the room checking on me. Then later he brought me dinner. I must say that it had improved over the last meal they gave me."

"Thanks," Marcia said with a smile. "I'm glad you liked it."

Gregg got the message. "So they drafted you into being cook. When you get away from here, I wouldn't blame you for not wanting to ever come back to Windcliff."

Marcia was quick to respond. "Oh, no. Don't say that. I love this house. Ever since I was a little girl I used to stand on the mainland cliffs watching Teal Island. Wondering what that beautiful house in the distance looked like from the inside."

Then Marcia reddened. She felt she shouldn't have said that. What would Gregg Spaniard think of her childish gushing? Gregg did not laugh at her.

Instead he said, "I'm glad you like Windcliff, Marcia. There have been times in the past when I wanted to ask a certain girl to come and see it. But she was always so aloof that I was afraid she might refuse my invitation."

The thought of Gregg having a girl somehow irritated Marcia. Then she realized she had no right to feel jealous. After all, Gregg did not belong to her.

"This girl, do I know her?" Marcia asked. "After all, Penwick is just a small town."

"Yes, you know her. She was three grades behind me in school. I found out that her father had been killed in an accident at sea. That she lived alone with her mother in a small house near the bay."

Marcia looked at Gregg and with the look that he returned she knew she was the girl he had been speaking of.

"I never thought of myself as being aloof. Determined, perhaps, but not aloof."

"In any event you finally made it to Windcliff. Only, this wasn't the way I had imagined it would be."

With those words they both became aware once more of the situation they were in. But somehow the atmosphere of the house had changed for Marcia. It no longer appeared threatening and menacing. Somehow she felt that she and Gregg would get out of this mess.

"If I could just get to a telephone," Gregg said. "I could call the authorities in Penwick."

"It's no use. The phone is dead. Brock said the storm had something to do with it."

An ironic smile touched Gregg's lips. "Brock probably had Joe cut the wires. We've had storms this bad before and communication was not cut off."

"What can we do? We can't just sit here and wait to see what happens."

Gregg paced the room. When he came to the French doors, he stopped.

"If we could make it to the boathouse, we could take one of the boats and go for help."

Marcia got up and walked over to where Gregg stood.

"That's a long drop to the ground. You might be able to make it. I know I can't. Why don't you try? I'll stay here. At least that way we might have a chance."

Gregg turned to look down on Marcia, his dark eyes heavy with concern.

"When I leave the island, it'll be with you. We can go over the balcony. All we have to do is tie some sheets together and drop them over the side. Only, we won't do it until after it gets dark. We're taking a big enough risk as it is."

"But what if Brock and the others decide to leave

this afternoon? What do you think they'll do with us?"

Deep lines formed between Gregg's thick eyebrows.

"I don't think they'll take a chance in leaving during the daylight hours. They don't want to attract any attention. And I feel that we're safe until they decide to leave."

Marcia couldn't help but heave a deep sigh.

"Then all we can do is wait. Am I right?"

Gregg put his hands on her shoulders. "I'm afraid that's all we can do."

After that they stood at the French doors, looking down at the bay that separated them from safety. There were a few sloops and ketches on the bay, their sails billowing with the force of the ever-present wind. If only there were some way to signal them.

"If we had a mirror, maybe we could send them a distress signal," Marcia said. Then she remembered her purse in the next room. "I'll be right back."

Before Gregg could protest, Marcia was on the railing of the balcony and leapt across the chasm separating the two balconies. She glanced back before she entered her room and saw the concerned look in Gregg's eyes.

Her purse was on the nightstand and Marcia hurriedly found the small mirror and clasped it in her right hand. Then she ran to the balcony and once more stepped onto the railing. She swayed uncertainly for a moment, getting her balance. Then, bending her knees, she leaped from the railing. As she landed on the floor of the opposite balcony, her right hand struck the railing of Gregg's balcony. The pain caused her to loosen her grip on the mirror and it fell from her grasp. There was a dull thud from below and Marcia looked down to see the mirror caught in the tangled growth of some shrubbery.

Gregg was at her side, helping her to her feet.

"Oh, Gregg, I'm sorry," she moaned.

Gregg's arms were about her, comforting her.

"You tried. It couldn't be helped. I should have gone in your place."

There was no time for further words. Below them they heard the sound of footsteps and Brock's voice carried to where they stood.

"I thought I heard something. Some racket out here."

"Ah, it's just your nerves," Evie said. "This place will give you the willies. How soon before we shuck this chamber of horrors?"

"You know the answer to that as well as I do. We have to wait for Racon's signal. In the meantime, I think I'll check on our guests upstairs."

"Any particular one in mind?" came Evie's sharp retort.

While they were bickering, Gregg led Marcia back inside the room. He headed for the chair he had been bound to and sat down.

"Hurry and tie me up, Marcia. When Brock comes in, I don't want him to suspect what's been going on."

Marcia went right to work doing the best she could with the ropes. Fortunately her father had taught her about tying knots so that in a short time Gregg was bound securely to the chair.

As she started toward the French doors, Gregg called to her, "You forgot the gag in my mouth."

Quickly, and with nervous hands, Marcia tied the thin strip of cloth behind Gregg's head. She touched his shoulder and he nodded his head in understanding. Then she scurried to the balcony, making certain she closed the doors behind her.

On the balcony, she hesitated, listening for the

sound of Evie and Brock's voices. Evidently they had finished their argument and had gone inside.

Marcia easily made it to her balcony and muttered to herself, "This is becoming a habit."

Shutting the French doors behind her, she grabbed the book by Dickens and sat on the nearest chair, opening the book at random. She started listening, straining her ears until she heard the sound of footsteps outside her room. With a great deal of effort she tried to focus her attention on the book as she heard the key inserted in the lock.

When the door was opened, she glanced up at Brock, who was looking at her with glacial eyes. He looked around the room. Then, without a word, he shut the door. In the silence that followed, Marcia could hear the key turning once more in the lock.

CHAPTER NINE

After Brock had gone, Marcia found that she was suddenly weary.

Why shouldn't I be? After all, look what's happened today, she thought. She walked to the bed and lay down with an exhausted sigh. It would be a good idea to get a little rest. Tonight's plan of escape would call for all the energy she could muster.

As she lay there, the events of the day swept across her mind like the tides of the bay. If she had not taken that path which led to the servants' quarters, she would not now be imprisoned in her room. In her mind she could still see the locked, boarded-up cottage. And she could feel the eyes of the watcher upon her. Now, she felt, it must have been Joe who had followed her movements. Still, she could not shake off the feeling that the watcher of Windcliff was someone else. Someone distant and not on the island.

Perhaps if she hadn't found the nurse's cap she would have been all right. Just what had become of Nurse Daniels? Was Brock so cruel that he had disposed of the nurse? He was quite capable of that, as was Joe. And Evie was so infatuated with Brock that she would be capable of following any order that Brock gave her.

They were such a strange group of people. Marcia

wondered why they were here. Gregg had discounted any suggestion that they were thieves. Yet what other motive could they possibly have for coming to Teal Island? Certainly Windcliff held valuable art and antique treasures. The house was a veritable thieves' paradise. But maybe it was hard cash they were after. Maybe they were waiting for their chance to find whatever money Joshia might have hidden away in the old house. That might explain why they were taking care of Joshia. They hoped that he might rally long enough to tell them where his money was kept.

Marcia tossed and turned on the bed. All she was doing was speculating. She really had no idea why Brock and the others had taken over Teal Island.

She thought of Gregg in the next room, bound and gagged and probably very uncomfortable. It had not been easy for her to tie the ropes about his body, but he had insisted. Thinking of Gregg, she felt a kind of warm assurance that they would be able to escape the island and Brock.

It had come as a pleasant surprise to learn that Gregg had noticed her throughout the years. Had even tried to get up enough courage to ask her to come visit Windcliff. Never had she thought that her love for him would be reciprocated. And she knew now that what she had felt for him all along was genuine. She did love Gregg and she felt that he felt that love for her.

A kind of tranquility settled over Marcia as she thought of Gregg, and she drifted off to sleep. A sleep that was surprisingly unmarred by the disturbing events of the past twenty-four hours.

Marcia awoke with Evie standing over her. She sat up rigidly in bed.

"Sorry to interrupt your beauty sleep, but Brock sent me up with some food."

Marcia glanced at her watch. It was six-thirty. She had really been pounding the pillow.

Evie set the tray down on the bed.

"Clam chowder! That smells good," Marcia said in a friendly tone of voice. "So you can cook, after all."

"Don't look at it too closely. With a can opener I can make my way around a kitchen."

Evie turned to go, but Marcia stopped her. "Do you have to go already? I haven't talked to anyone all afternoon. Can't you stay for a few minutes?"

Evie sighed. "Well, I guess I could use a little break. I'll have a cigarette while you eat."

Fumbling in her pocket, Evie brought out a crumpled pack of cigarettes. She lighted one, then sat on the vanity bench.

Marcia took a sip of the chowder. The best that could be said about it was that it was hot. "Oh, this hits the spot," she lied.

Evie exhaled a blue stream of smoke. "You're easily pleased. I thought it tasted terrible. I can hardly wait to get off this island and have a real meal."

"There's a great seafood restaurant in Penwick," Marcia said, trying to be casual about her conversation.

Evie snorted, "You can have your seafood. I'm talking about a steak with potatoes smothered with sour cream and chives. I know a great place in Denver that serves fabulous meals. Used to work there. Won't the manager be surprised when I come in as a customer. That'll be a hoot."

Marcia wanted to keep Evie talking. She just might reveal some important information. "So you and Brock will be going to Denver when you leave here. I've never been there."

Evie relaxed, leaning back against the dressing

table. Again Marcia noticed that Evie would have been a very attractive person if she hadn't gone in so heavily for the cosmetics.

Evie began to talk, telling Marcia about her childhood. It wasn't a very pleasant story. Her father had been a tyrant and quite brutal. He beat Evie and her brothers and sisters for no apparent reason. When she was sixteen, she had left home and gotten a job as a car hop. From there she drifted across the country, working long enough to save up a little money and then moving on. She was working in a small restaurant when she met Brock.

"The day I met Brock, I knew my luck was changing. He told me about this deal he was working on. He said that when it was over, we'd have enough money to live in grand style for a long time."

"Sounds really great," Marcia said. "But I cant see that Windcliff has all that much to offer in the way of big money. Sure, it has some valuable paintings and antiques, but they would be hard to dispose of."

"Who said anything about paintings and antiques?" Evie said, snuffing out her cigarette. "I'm talking about big money. And it has nothing to do with this junk at Windcliff."

Marcia winced at the way Evie put down all the beautiful furnishings. Yet at the same time she was relieved that Brock had no intention of looting the house.

Evie got to her feet. "I got to get a move on. Besides, I think you make me talk too much. And that isn't healthy for me or you."

"What do you mean by that?" Marcia asked anxiously.

"Just take my word for it. Brock can be a gentleman at times. But don't let that fool you."

Evie picked up the tray and without a backward glance quickly strolled out of the room. Once the door was shut, there came the ominious clicking of the key in the lock.

Marcia had gotten no nearer a friendship with Evie than before. And she had not learned anything, except that robbery was not the underlying reason for Brock Janis's appearance at Windcliff.

It would not be long until sunset, but to Marcia the minutes dragged into hours. She paced the room, pausing now and then to watch the sunlight fade on the choppy waters of the bay.

Across the bay she could see the first sprinkling of lights in Penwick. She idly wondered what Adam Long was doing at that moment. This was the first time he had come into her thoughts since she had met Gregg Spaniard. Adam had made known his intentions and had suggested before he left for New York that he would be seeing more of Marcia.

Although Adam had many fine qualities, she did not feel any quickening of the heart as was the case when she was near Gregg. Adam could never be any more than a friend. She would make that clear to him once she saw him again. But when would that be?

Marcia would not allow herself to think negative thoughts, so she brushed them aside as she watched the last rays of the sun touch the milky whitecaps in the bay.

Before she knew it, night had fallen. With the enshrouding darkness came the quiet that crept over the house. The only sound was the faraway crashing of waves against the rocky shore. She wondered if one ever got accustomed to the noise of the breakers. You would have to if you lived on this remote island.

Now that the room had become darkened, Marcia wondered whether or not to turn on the lights. If she did not, that might attract attention more than a lighted room. She switched on the bedside lamp, which gave out just enough light to avert suspicion.

She had heard the door to Gregg's room open shortly after Evie had left her. Gregg had been served his chowder and then the door had been shut and locked.

By this time, Brock, Evie, and Joe would be in the downstairs area of the house. Marcia cautiously opened the French doors and stepped onto the balcony. A pale moon cast weird shadows on the lawn below and threw silver streamers across the restless waters of Penwick Bay.

There was no light visible in Gregg's room. How cruel Brock was to not only truss up Gregg but also leave him in a darkened room.

Marcia peered over the banister of the balcony to make sure her actions were not seen. Then she bounded over the balcony, landing expertly on her feet.

The doors to Gregg's room were unlocked and she quickly made her way inside. She waited a moment until her eyes became accustomed to the dark. Then she saw Gregg still bound to the chair where she had left him earlier that day. With quick strides, Marcia was at his side and gingerly attacked the ropes after she had slid the gag from his mouth.

"You don't know how good it is to see you," Gregg said. "I've done nothing but think about you all afternoon. It kept my sanity."

Hearing Gregg speak these words made Marcia's pulse race. She did not know whether she should tell him that he had been on her mind also that afternoon.

Instead she said, "I heard Evie come here earlier. Did she suspect anything?"

Gregg was massaging his wrists. "I don't think so.

Anyway, you were better at tying me up than Brock was. Where did you learn to handle ropes like that?"

"You forget my father was a fisherman. He never treated me like I was an only child. If there was any work to be done on his boat, he let me help."

A wide grin split Gregg's full lips. "You are constantly amazing, Marcia Carpenter. For such a slight girl, you are amazingly hardy."

Marcia laughed. "You can thank my mother for that. I inherited her tenacity. Some people might even call it stubbornness."

"You don't give up easily. I like that in a person," Gregg said, walking toward a closet where he brought out some sheets. "This may not be too easy a way to climb down from the balcony, but I think we can do it."

Gregg tied two sheets securely together and then went out on the balcony. Marcia watched as he cautiously lowered the sheets over the side to see how close they came to the ground. "It will be a slight drop. The sheets are a few feet short."

Marcia made no comment so Gregg quickly tied one end of the sheets to the railing. Looking down, Marcia swallowed a lump in her throat. She would not let Gregg know that the prospect of lowering herself on the sheets was not very appealing to her. There was no other way of being free of the house. She could not back out now.

"I'll go first," Gregg said. "Just watch how I do it. I'll be down there waiting for you."

Gregg slipped effortlessly over the balcony railing, grabbing the dangling sheets with his hands. It looked so easy as he moved hand below hand to lower himself to the garden. Then he had to jump down a short distance.

For a moment Marcia stood leaning over the balcony. It seemed a long way down to where Gregg stood looking up at her. He motioned with his hand, not daring to raise his voice.

Taking a deep breath of air, Marcia eased one leg over the balcony as she held tightly to the makeshift ladder. Once she had a firm grip, she raised the other leg and felt herself suspended in the air. She fought the panic that was sweeping over her body.

Don't look down, she told herself as she cautiously began lowering her body from the balcony. Halfway down, a sudden gust of wind swept over her, and she spun helplessly in its face. She was tempted to cry out, but all she could think of was to hold on tightly. The wind subsided and Marcia once again commenced her descent.

Coming to the end of the sheets, she released her grip and dropped into Gregg's waiting arms. She clung to him, needing the assurance that his strong arms offered her.

"You did that like a professional," Gregg said with a low chuckle.

"I don't think I want to make a life's work out of it," Marcia replied, her sense of humor returning.

"If you're all right, we'd better get a move on. But first I'll try and cover up our tracks."

Gregg took the end of the dangling sheets and with a quick movement of his wrists sent the sheets upward where they disappeared over the balcony railing.

"Let's go," Gregg whispered as he gently but firmly clasped Marcia by the arm. As they started to move, a blinding light suddenly shattered the darkness. "Quick, we'll hide behind that bush," Gregg said, thrusting Marcia ahead of him.

The light had come from the French doors below

Gregg's balcony. Marcia was in a crouched position behind the shrubbery and her line of vision was cut off. She could hear her heart pounding in her ears.

A door opened and she heard the sound of footsteps come nearer and nearer. As they reached the bushes, she heard Evie's voice from the opened French doors. "What's the matter?"

Brock was so near, Marcia felt she could reach out and touch him. "I thought I heard something," he said.

At that moment a blast of wind rattled the open French doors.

"You just heard the wind. Come on back inside, Brock."

Brock hesitated for what seemed an eternity. Then he turned and walked back toward the house. "I guess you're right. This place is beginning to get on my nerves."

"What you need is a brandy," said Evie as their voices trailed off with the closing of the French doors.

Gregg and Marcia waited in their cramped positions until the light was switched off and they were once more in the protection of the darkness.

Without waiting a minute longer, Gregg helped Marcia to her feet, and then they hurried along the pathway to the boathouse.

CHAPTER TEN

"Stay close behind me," Gregg said in his natural voice. They were far enough from Windcliff so that their voices would not carry in the wind. "I know this path like the back of my hand. But it can be tricky to a newcomer."

Marcia had no intention of straying one inch from Gregg. She was still shaking from their near encounter with Brock Janis. If he had only come a few steps nearer...but he hadn't, so she just had to rid her mind of the danger that was past. Thank heavens Evie had inadvertently come to their aid. Marcia hoped that Joe was still inside the house. He, of all people, she didn't want to meet on this narrow pathway.

Clouds were scudding across the sky, throwing the island into quick shadows as they passed over the face of the moon. When the moon did rid itself of the clouds, Marcia could see ahead to where the path wound its way among the rocky cliffs.

Gregg was deliberately going at a slow pace so that Marcia could keep up with him. In the intermittent moonlight she saw how wide and strong his shoulders were and she felt safe and secure as she hurried behind him.

As they moved along the twisting pathway, Marcia suddenly thought of Joshia alone in his room. If Brock and Evie discovered that she and Gregg were gone before they could return with help, would they harm the old man? In her haste to get away from Brock and his cohorts, she had completely forgotten Joshia.

"Gregg, I've been thinking about your father," she began, but Gregg interrupted her.

"I know. So have I. Brock may be a pretty shady character, but I doubt if he'll harm him. Dad can't move or speak, so he's no threat to them. And they may not have a chance to do anything if they don't discover we're gone."

Hearing Gregg speak so reassuringly made Marcia feel better. She glanced behind her and saw the house framed against the dark night sky. A few lights were blazing in the windows, which told her where Brock, Evie, and Joe were. It saddened her somewhat to have had her dreams of Windcliff dashed because of the trio. Maybe, when this was all over, she might be asked to return to Teal Island under more happy circumstances. That thought cheered her and she turned her attention once more to the twisting path.

The crash of the angry waves below had grown louder as they had neared the high cliffs. Gregg's stride had quickened as though the restless tides were awakening some urgency in him.

They had arrived at a natural stairway carved from the granite rocks of the cliffs. There was no railing to hold on to, and the steps were slick from yesterday's rain and the constant spray of seawater borne by the wind.

Halfway down the steep stairway, Marcia slipped and Gregg, hearing the sound, spun around and caught her before she fell.

"Are you all right?" he said in a concerned voice.

"I just lost my balance. You never know how

dependent you are on railings until you don't have one to cling to."

"There was a wooden railing at one time, when Windcliff was first built. During the years it gave way, and we had it torn down. Dad and I had planned on putting up a metal one. We just never got around to it."

Gregg released his hold and turned to continue his descent. Marcia followed cautiously, now aware of the danger that the stairway presented. She would be glad when they would be down at the bottom.

Once she glanced to her right and saw the tip of the boathouse roof. They had made a lot of progress since climbing down from Gregg's room. The boathouse should be just around the cliff.

The stairway ended abruptly and Marcia found herself on porous, rock-strewn land. The boathouse was only a few feet away. When the moon came out from behind a cloud, she could see two huge doors. The structure appeared to be deserted.

Gregg paused, taking in the sight as though he were making sure there was no one guarding the boathouse. Then he moved slowly, cautiously, forward. Marcia was beside him now, anxious to see what was inside the building.

When they got to the double doors, Gregg said, "That's odd. There was a lock on that hasp. It would appear that our guests were curious about the boats inside. I don't like the looks of that."

Before Marcia could say anything, Gregg slowly opened the double doors. The hinges squeaked and Gregg paused, looking back at Windcliff.

"I doubt that they'll be able to hear us, but I don't want to be overconfident," he said as he eased the doors the rest of the way back.

Faint moonlight shone dimly on the interior of the boathouse, but Marcia could see several boats of various sizes and shapes; everything from a catamaran to a cabin cruiser. Gregg headed toward the nearest boat, a runabout.

It was just a short distance to where the waves dashed upon the shoreline and Gregg expertly maneuvered the small craft, with Marcia's help, into the water.

As Gregg assisted her aboard, Marcia shivered, vividly recalling her fear of the water.

"Are you okay?" Gregg asked as he held one of her trembling hands.

Marcia began telling him of her fear of the water. The words poured out of her between tears and gasping sobs. Gregg listened quietly, allowing her to let it all out. She had never told anyone of her terror before, not even her mother. All the anguish she had stored away since the death of her father now came rushing out in a torrent of words.

When she had finished, she found that she was in Gregg's arms. He held her tenderly and stroked her head with one of his hands.

"Do you feel better?" he asked as her tears began to subside.

Strangely, Marcia did. Now that her fears had been brought out in the open, they did not seem like such dreadful specters. She dried her eyes as Gregg sat quietly beside her.

"I'm fine now. That was silly of me. As if we didn't have enough troubles without me acting like a ninny."

Gregg smiled at her. "I like that, what you just said."

Marcia looked at Gregg, not understanding what he was talking about. "What do you mean?"

"About us having troubles. Not just you or me. But us."

At that moment, a light went on in the upper floor of Windcliff. Both Marcia and Gregg saw the light at the same time.

"That must be Brock checking on us," Gregg said as he moved toward the bow of the runabout. "We'd better get a move on."

Then Marcia saw another light come on in another room. Whoever was up there must have discovered that they were both gone.

She turned quickly. "Gregg, I think they've found out we're both gone. I just saw lights come on in another room of the house."

The boat, unanchored, had begun to drift quite a distance into the bay. The dark, cold water of the bay rocked the small craft showering Marcia with briny sea spray.

She heard Gregg trying to start the motor, but there was no response. Then she heard him slam his fist against the steering mechanism.

"What's wrong, Gregg?" Marcia asked.

"I knew things were going too good. They figured we might try to make a break for it. So they took precautionary measures."

"Precautionary measures?" Marcia asked.

Gregg turned toward her, his face a mixture of anger and disgust.

"They drained all the gas tanks. Joe probably did it when he was checking on the boats. That's why we found the boathouse unlocked. They didn't have anything to worry about. We walked right into their trap."

A feeling of dread began to grow in the pit of Marcia's stomach. They had underestimated Brock Janis. Without any gasoline they would drift helplessly in the bay, at the mercy of the wind and the waves. Their avenue of escape had been cut off.

"Don't you keep an extra supply of gas, just in case of emergencies?" Marcia asked.

"I checked that. They even got rid of our auxiliary tank."

Marcia grasped the wooden railing of the vessel as a spray of water swept over her. They were continuing to drift farther and farther from the shore. Her feet were beginning to get damp and she shivered in the night air. She wondered why there was so much water in the boat. Surely it couldn't come from the faint spray, could it? Then she glanced down at her feet. The entire bottom of the runabout was now covered with an inch of water. Something was wrong.

"Gregg! Look at all the water that's in the boat. Where is it all coming from?"

Gregg was on his feet immediately. He moved from the steering mechanism and dropped to his knees, frantically touching the hull of the boat with his hands. Marcia knew that he was looking for the source of the leakage.

Even as he moved about on his hands and knees, Marcia could see the water level rising steadily in the small craft.

Gregg got to his feet. "They went all the way. If the gasoline didn't stop us, a hole in the boat would. We're taking on water fast, Marcia."

Marcia was immobilized with fear. The sea which had once claimed her father was now reaching out for her. She moved her feet in the water which by now was above her ankles. The water was ice cold, chilling her to the marrow of her bones. Her hands clutched the railing of the boat as if there was some safety in that gesture.

Gregg sloshed through the water and was at her side. His voice seemed to come from a faraway tunnel.

"We'll have to swim to shore, Marcia. The boat's sinking fast. We have to abandon ship."

Marcia heard him speak, but her mind would not grasp what he was saying. Her hands dug into the railing until her fingers ached with agonizing pain.

"Marcia!" Gregg was shouting. "Do you hearwhat I'm saying?"

A sudden wave struck the small boat, showering Marcia with its dampness. It was like a slap in the face. Marcia relaxed her grip.

"But, Gregg, I've never learned to swim," Marcia said in a frightened voice.

"Hold onto me. And don't panic, even if your head goes under the water for a second. Do you understand?"

Marcia nodded.

Gregg slipped over the side of the runabout. For a moment the sea appeared to swallow him up and Marcia gasped. Then his head reappeared and he reached out his strong arms for her.

Summoning all the courage she could, Marcia started over the side of the small craft. She saw the waves lapping at the boat, dark and unfathomable. Midway Marcia froze. She could not loosen her grip on the railing.

Gregg saw the fear and terror in Marcia's face and he began talking to her in a calm, comforting voice.

"It's going to be all right, Marcia. I'm here. I won't let anything happen to you. And it's not that far. Do you trust me?"

When Gregg spoke those words, it seemed to banish all her fears. Yes, she did trust Gregg. She loved him and she felt he loved her. He wouldn't let anything harm her. Strengthened by that trusting love, she calmly slipped over the side of the boat into Gregg's waiting arms.

Gregg maneuvered her about in the chilly water until she was behind him with her arms entwined about his shoulders. "Now, whatever happens, darling, don't let go. Promise me?"

"I promise," Marcia said, holding onto Gregg's broad shoulders with all her might.

Then Gregg began to move through the choppy waters of the bay. The moon had disappeared completely behind a heavy bank of clouds. Ahead of them stood Windcliff with its lights blazing in the darkness. Gregg kept his eyes focused on the shore and the outline of Windcliff.

The water was cold, numbing. Marcia felt her arms weakening around Gregg's neck, but she held on. She forced her mind to think of other things, to keep her thoughts from the predicament they were in. Gregg had called her darling. That word alone gave her renewed strength. She had to make it to shore. Gregg's love would get them there.

The current was against them, but Gregg's powerful arms cut through the dark waters slowly drawing them nearer the shore.

Marcia's arms had no feeling in them and her body had a pleasant drowsiness that frightened her. Then Gregg stopped swimming. He had touched bottom. Gradually he eased Marcia's arms from around his neck and picked her up tenderly. He carried her to shore and placed her gently on the grainy sand.

"We made it. You were terrific," Gregg said as he began rubbing her hands until feeling came back in them.

Marcia was trembling, shaking all over from the wetness of the water.

"There's a blanket in the boathouse. You need something to warm you," he said as he dashed away.

Marcia's teeth were chattering and her whole body was one big shiver. She watched as Gregg sprinted to the boathouse and emerged with a blanket. When he had wrapped it around her, its warmth stopped her shaking.

"There's nothing like a moonlight swim to refresh you," Marcia said, and Gregg threw back his head as he laughed.

"Believe it or not, I sometimes take moonlight swims. I never realized what I was missing when I swam alone."

Marcia used a portion of the blanket to dry her hair. She was glad she wore it cut so short.

For a while they sat on the shore looking out at the bay. The runabout had disappeared, undoubtedly at the bottom of the bay.

Marcia said regretfully, "I'm sorry about the boat, Gregg."

Gregg gave a deep sigh. "Thank God you're all right. Brock Janis nearly killed us both. The only thing is, we aren't any nearer getting help than we were before."

Behind them came the sound of voices being carried along the wind. Gregg sprang to his feet.

"We aren't out of danger yet. They're coming to look for us. If they see that one of the boats is gone, they'll assume we drowned."

Marcia was on her feet, hugging the blanket to her body. "What will we do, Gregg? Where can we hide?"

"There's a place I know. A cave I used to stay in

sometimes when I was a kid. Sort of a hideout. They'll never find us there. Are you rested enough to make a run for it?"

"You lead the way," Marcia said with determination. "I'll keep up with you."

CHAPTER ELEVEN

Gregg and Marcia ran desperately between the high cliffs, pausing now and then to make certain they were not being followed. Above them the dark clouds had thickened and the wind had increased its force, a sure indication that another storm was about to break.

Marcia had discarded the blanket because it hampered her running. She was too intent on escaping from Brock and Joe to think about being tired.

When they had gone a great distance, Gregg pulled Marcia into the shelter of an overhanging cliff. Here they hid, catching their breath. After a time they emerged and stood for a moment looking back at the distance they had covered. The boathouse was hidden from view and Marcia saw they had approached the east side of Windcliff.

"Where is the hiding place, Gregg? Is it far?"

"We still have a way to go. From here on, we can take it easy. Brock probably thinks we went down with the boat."

Even though the words had a chilling sound, Marcia was relieved that they could slacken their speed. From what Gregg had said, the cave was still some distance away and they had time to reach it. Still, they walked briskly along the pathway Gregg had chosen.

A fine rain had begun to fall adding to Marcia's already soaked condition. But surprisingly the rain did not dampen her spirits. She could have walked through the eye of a hurricane if Gregg were at her side. It was Gregg who said he was glad it had begun to rain.

"Pardon me for asking, but why did you say that?" Marcia asked. "Haven't we both had enough soaking for one night?"

Gregg chuckled. "That's for sure. But we need the rain to wash away our footprints. They would lead Brock right to us in the morning."

Marcia had to agree that Gregg was right. It made it easier to move forward when she knew that each footprint she made would be eventually washed away by the rain. The less they had to worry about being discovered by Brock and Joe, the better for them.

She hadn't realized Teal Island was as large as it was. All the time she had watched the island from her lookout at Penwick she had never thought of the island as being particularly big. Now that she had been forced to walk around it, she was beginning to realize how her eyes had misjudged that cluster of rocks in Penwick Bay.

"Can we rest for a moment, Gregg?" Marcia said as they approached a gathering of odd-shaped rocks. "I'm about played out."

Gregg put an arm around her shoulders and said, "Do you think you can make it to that rock formation?"

Marcia nodded.

"Good. That's where we'll rest. In my hideout."

Marcia almost sobbed she was so relieved to hear those words. The dampness of the night, the harrowing escape from the sinking boat, plus the flight from Brock—they were all beginning to take their toll. She let Gregg guide her as they entered a shaft that was concealed between two overhanging boulders.

Once they were inside, Gregg took her hand to lead her. It was so dark in the tunnel that Marcia could not see her hand in front of her face. But dark or not, she was grateful to be safe from the rain outside.

Their footsteps were muffled as they moved cautiously along the serpentine tunnel which to Marcia appeared to descend into the heart of the island. The cold of the rain had been replaced by the chill of the cave and Marcia shivered in the unrelieved darkness.

"Don't give up, we're just about there," Gregg said, and Marcia wondered how he could see anything in this dank place.

But in a few minutes the walls of the tunnel widened and she could sense that they had entered a wide room.

"Now, if memory serves, I think there is a lantern to my right." Gregg moved away, leaving Marcia alone. She fought the desire to call out to him knowing that it would make her sound like a frightened child. Then Gregg struck a match, touched it to the wick of a lantern. Instantly the shadows fled and Marcia looked at her surroundings.

They were in a small room, perfectly formed by some long-ago pocket of gas when the earth was cooling. Along one wall were shelves of canned goods, and a few chairs were scattered about the floor. A wobbly table stood in the center of the room, and there was even a crude fireplace with a smoke-blackened wall where years ago Gregg must have had a fire blazing.

"It's not fancy, but at least we're out of the elements," Gregg said as he placed the lantern on the rickety table.

"You couldn't have chosen a better place, Gregg. It's perfect," Marcia said, inspecting the supply of food.

"Take your pick. I'll get a fire going. We don't have to worry about anyone seeing the smoke on a night like this."

While Marcia looked over the canned goods, Gregg got a fire started in the fireplace. It wasn't long before the warmth from the blazing logs took the chill off the room.

Marcia found an old kettle and coffeepot and some eating utensils covered with a plastic wrapping to keep the dust off them.

She set the table and opened a can of beans, which she poured into the kettle. Placing the kettle over the fire, she said, "If we had some water, we could have coffee. I found the coffee and a pot, but no water."

"No sooner said than done," Gregg said, walking to a darkened corner of the room and tossing back a tarp. A huge wooden barrel stood exposed and Gregg turned on the spigot, filling the pot with water. Evidently, fresh rainwater was somehow piped to the barrel.

"You thought of everything when you found this hideout," Marcia said. "All the comforts of Wind-cliff."

Gregg watched as Marcia ladled some coffee into the pot. "You forget that I spent a lot of time here when I was growing up. As an only child I had to create my own amusements. The day I found this cave I felt like Ali Baba. I used to do a lot of thinking and dreaming inside these stone walls."

Listening to Gregg speak of his childhood brought Marcia back to her own with a sudden nostalgia. They were so alike in so many ways. Gregg had been reared without a mother, and her father had been taken from her early in her life. Each of them was an only child.

The aroma of fresh-perked coffee filled the air with a tantalizing fragrance. Marcia found two mugs and filled them to the brim. She motioned to Gregg to continue with his story as she curled up by the fire. The crackling flames, the snugness of the cave, temporarily made her forget the dire circumstances that faced them on the outside.

"After school I returned to Teal Island and Dad went over the responsibilities and financial situation of the Spaniard fortune. He had Adam Long draw up papers authorizing me to be legally responsible. That was just before he had the stroke."

Marcia was so engrossed in listening to Gregg that she almost forgot about the beans simmering on the hearth, until she sniffed the air. She jumped to her feet and, grabbing a pot holder, pulled the kettle from the fire.

"I got so carried away I almost forgot about our food," she apologized.

Gregg opened a tin of biscuits as Marcia filled their plates.

"That smells delicious. Boy, what you can do with a can of beans."

"I hope it's as good as Evie's tuna-fish sandwiches," Marcia said wryly.

Gregg made a face. "Don't mention Evie's food. Not while I'm eating."

They both laughed, the sound reverberating off the smooth walls of the cave. When they had finished, Gregg said, "The lucky guy that marries you!"

Marcia glanced at him. His dark hair was gleaming in the light from the blazing logs.

"There is a lucky guy at Penwick," he said. "Isn't there?"

"At the moment, no," Marcia answered, remembering, if Gregg didn't, that earlier that evening he had called her darling. She saw the relieved look on Gregg's face.

But at the moment Marcia did not think they should pursue this direction of talk. Considering the circumstances they were in and their surroundings. She reached inside the pocket of her dress and felt the plastic sack that she had found on the cellar steps.

"I almost forgot about this. It must be either sugar or salt. I found it on the cellar steps."

She opened the plastic bag and sniffed it. Then she made a face. "This isn't sugar or salt."

"Let me see that," Gregg said, reaching for the plastic bag.

After examining it, Gregg looked intently at Marcia. "I think you've accidentally discovered the reason Brock and his cohorts are on Teal Island."

"What do you mean?" Marcia asked. "What's in that bag, Gregg?"

"Some kind of drug," Gregg said as he dropped the plastic sack on the table.

"You mean Brock is dealing in dope?" Marcia gasped.

"It looks that way. Why else would this stuff be lying around? Brock or Joe must have dropped it when they were hauling the stuff into the house. It's probably stored in the cellar."

Marcia couldn't take her eyes off the innocent-appearing white powder.

"Do you think Brock, Evie, and Joe use it?"

Gregg shrugged. "I doubt it. I'm inclined to think they are just smuggling the stuff into the country."

"But why did they stop here on the island? Why didn't they just take it on to the mainland?"

"All I can figure out is that they're just part of a ring. They must be waiting for the head of the syndicate to get in touch with them. Then they'll make the contact and whoever is the head of the organization will pay them."

"Then they must have been watching Teal Island waiting for their chance to use Windcliff as a stopover."

Gregg nodded.

"It wouldn't take too much planning to figure out that Windcliff was an ideal setup for them. Brock probably knew that Dad was sick and that with the element of surprise on their side they could easily move in."

Marcia was thinking. Something was nagging at the back of her mind. Something she had overheard recently.

"Racon. We heard Brock mention the name Racon, remember? He told Evie they had to wait for a signal from Racon. What do you suppose that means?"

Gregg slapped his hand against the table.

"Racon must be who their contact is. That's why they've been so patient. They won't make an effort to move the drugs until Racon contacts them."

"Then as soon as Racon contacts them, they'll be gone."

Marcia thought what that would mean. If they could just hold out long enough, Brock and Joe and Evie would be gone. A feeling of hope surged through Marcia to disappear when she thought of the consequences of Brock's leaving the island.

"Gregg, do you realize what it will mean if they go with that stuff?"

"I sure do. I'm thinking about all the people who'll get a hold of that junk and what it will do to them."

Marcia refilled their mugs with coffee and they sat in silence as they warmed their hands on the heat from the mugs.

Lost in her thoughts, Marcia was startled when Gregg said, "There's nothing we can do tonight about Brock. Maybe we'll come up with a plan tomorrow. Worry won't do us any good."

"I guess you're right," Marcia said with a yawn. She was suddenly very tired. The events of the day were beginning to tell on her.

"You've had it," Gregg said. "I think it's time for you to get some sleep."

Marcia watched with drooping eyelids as Gregg rummaged through an old chest and came up with two sleeping bags. The cave had many curved indentations whose depths were swallowed up with dark shadows. Taking the lantern, Gregg went to the niche nearest the fireplace and spread out a sleeping bag.

"This is where you sleep, Marcia. It's close to the fire, so you'll stay warm. I'll sleep across the room so I can keep an eye on the entrance."

Marcia was too tired to argue. She crept into the sleeping bag and Gregg zipped up the side. He squatted beside her and said, "I'll throw some more wood on the fire, so it will last the night. Will you be all right?"

"Remind me to thank the manager in the morning for such good service," Marcia said with a faint smile.

"You're a good sport," Gregg said as he got to his feet and began feeding more wood to the fire.

Marcia was drowsy. She saw Gregg's shadow waver across the far wall as he moved before the flickering flame of the fire. The sleeping bag was cozy and warm. Her eyelids were heavy and she fought a losing battle to stay awake.

Inside the cave, all sounds of the rain and the wind and even the crashing of the waves were muted in the distance, lulling her into a deep sleep.

As tired as she was, Marcia still could not help thinking of Windcliff and the problems that had arisen since she had arrived. It had only been a short time ago that she had stepped off the boat, but so much had happened in that brief span of time.

She had been right when her instinct had told her that Brock Janis could not be Gregg's cousin. There was no way that a despicable person like Brock Janis could be related to such a gentle, considerate man as Gregg. Thinking of Gregg, Marcia smiled faintly.

Before she drifted off to sleep, she thought of Adam Long. If only he had not gone away, he would be concerned about her and maybe have come to their aid. But if Adam hadn't gone to New York, she wouldn't have had the opportunity to come to Windcliff. Even with all the dreadful things that had happened to her, she was thankful that she had met Gregg. They would find a way tomorrow to prevent Brock from delivering his cargo. Together the two of them would think up something.

When she did at last sleep, she had disturbing dreams. She found herself once more in the halls of Windcliff. Gregg was calling to her and she was facing a corridor of locked rooms. In her hands was a ring of keys. As she tried each door, she found only an empty, cold room. Gregg's voice became fainter and she hurried frantically to unlock the seemingly endless row of doors. At last she came to the final door. With trembling hands she tried the key and the door was flung open. Instead of finding Gregg there, she found Brock Janis with a mocking smile on his lips.

Marcia awoke with a start. For a moment she stared at the unfamiliar surroundings. Gradually, she remembered where she was. The flames had died down considerably in the fireplace, but they still gave some light and the cave still retained its warmth.

Marcia unzipped the bag and slowly slipped out. She got unsteadily to her feet and looked around the shadowy room. Beyond the table and chairs she saw the other sleeping bag. But there was something wrong. She could tell from where she stood that it was unoccupied. Gregg was gone.

CHAPTER TWELVE

Never had Marcia felt so forsaken and alone. She stood there, unable to believe that Gregg had deserted her. Once, a long time ago, her father had taken her on a walk and she had gotten lost. It had only been for a few minutes and her father had come rushing to her side, sweeping her up into his strong arms while she wept frightened tears. Marcia felt that same feeling standing here in the shadowy cave, somewhat frightened and terribly alone.

You're a grown woman now, pull yourself together, she chided herself, which did a lot to bolster her sagging morale. Squaring her shoulders, she walked purposefully over to the sleeping bag. She hadn't been mistaken. It lay flat, with the top flap thrown back just as Gregg had left it when he obviously had decided to go wherever it was.

Marcia picked up the lantern and struck a match to the wick. Even though she felt it must be daylight outside, the cave was fairly dark. She didn't know what to do. Should she try to find Gregg? No, she knew it would be best to wait for him here in the cave. He was sure to come back. He just had to!

To keep her mind occupied, she got busy straightening up the room and even put some coffee on the dying fire to heat. Before long the aroma of coffee filled the air, dispelling the gloom of the primitive shelter.

As Marcia took a cup and poured it full of coffee, a voice said, "Smells good. Nothing like a cup of coffee to start the day."

Marcia almost dropped the coffeepot as she whirled to see Gregg standing at the entrance to the main part of the cave. He had just returned, through the twisting tunnel. Without thinking, she put the cup and pot on the table and ran to him. He took her into his strong arms. "This is even better than coffee," he laughed.

"Oh, Gregg, I was so worried about you. When I woke up and found that you were gone, I didn't know what to think."

Gregg held her at arm's length. There was a tender look in his dark eyes. "I'm glad that you were concerned about me. But I left you a note. Didn't you read it?"

"Note? I didn't find a note?"

Gregg put an arm around her and they both walked to the table. "Here it is," he said as he picked up a scrap of paper and handed it to her. She felt foolish and quickly glanced at the words that said Gregg would be gone for only a short time and not to worry. She crumpled the note and tossed it into the fire.

"How about a cup of coffee?" she said to change the subject.

"Great. I believe there are some cookies in one of those tins."

Gregg opened a tin and handed Marcia a cookie that surprisingly was not stale. As Gregg took a sip of coffee, he looked around. "Just what this place needed, a woman's touch."

Marcia brushed the remark aside. "Did you go to Windcliff? I have no idea what time it is. My watch stopped when we were in the water. Is it daylight outside?"

"Yes, to both questions. You were sleeping so soundly I didn't want to wake you. It was still dark when I went to the house. Everybody was still asleep. So I came back here for you."

Marcia swallowed a bite of the cookie. "Are we going back to the house?"

"I want to check the cellar just to be sure that what we suspect is true. It might be dangerous. If you would rather wait here, I'll understand."

Looking around at the bleak surroundings, it didn't take Marcia very long to make her decision. "I'm going with you."

Gregg reached out and touched her hand. "Good. I knew you were a spunky gal. We'll get started as soon as we finish eating."

Marcia sipped the hot liquid. She felt her strength returning and with it a determination. There had to be a way for them to get help. She had no idea how that would come about, yet she felt things would work out for the two of them. That kind of thinking she knew had come from her mother, a positive and optimistic woman.

"I keep thinking about Adam Long. Maybe he finished with his business in New York sooner than he thought. He might be in Penwick at this very moment, wondering what happened to me."

Gregg removed his hand from hers. "You think a lot of Adam Long, don't you?"

"He gave me my first job. I owe a great deal to him," Marcia said, gazing into Gregg's dark eyes. At the mention of Adam Long, she had seen a flicker of annoyance in them. Then that look passed as swiftly as it had come.

"You're a very loyal person. Adam Long is a good man."

"And a good friend," Marcia added. She couldn't help noticing the relieved look that came over Gregg's face at those words.

Then she said, "I hope your father is all right, that they haven't harmed him in any way."

"I've been thinking about him too. Brock Janis may be a crook and a scoundrel, but I seriously doubt that he would harm a defenseless old man. And Evie seems to have taken a liking to Dad. At least she'll see that he gets fed."

When they had finished eating, Gregg got to his feet.

"Are you ready?"

Marcia nodded.

Gregg went to a corner of the room and opened an old duffle bag. He reached inside and brought out a faded cardigan sweater. "Put this on. It will keep you warm. There's still a morning chill outside."

The sweater smelled musty, but its warmth felt good as Marcia slipped it on. Gregg extinguished the light in the lantern and the room became shadowy, illuminated only by the last embers of the fire.

Marcia looked around at the cave with a feeling of anxiety at leaving its safety. In the short time she had been here, she had felt cut off from the danger that threatened her outside. The cave had been a safe port in the storm. But Gregg was waiting for her. She hurried to his side.

Now that she had once been through the serpentine, twisting tunnel, she walked more easily between its walls. Gregg stayed a short distance ahead and though she could only faintly see him, she felt his reassuring presence. Gradually the faint outline of his body grew more distinct and a faint shimmer of light like an aureole surrounded him. Ahead, Marcia could hear the crashing of the surf against the rugged shoreline, and the air was filled with the tang of iodine. There was no sound of rain, but the wind moaned icily as they approached the entrance to the cave.

It was daylight outside, with a faint mist that obscured the mainland. Penwick was still sleeping under a damp bank of fog. For the first time Marcia did not feel those watchful eyes upon her. That was probably because Brock, Evie, and Joe were still pounding the pillows.

"I think we'll take the same trail we used last night. There is a cutoff a little way down the beach where we can get to the house without being seen."

Marcia shivered slightly in the chill morning in spite of the sweater. "I'm glad you know all about Teal Island. If it were up to me, I'd be lost in no time. You said it didn't appear that anybody was awake at Windcliff."

Gregg nodded.

"Right. They probably think we're in a watery grave."

Marcia's trembling intensified at that remark.

"But that's to our advantage," he went on. "They won't be expecting us to come prowling around the house."

For a moment the sun cut through the fog and its warm rays felt good. Her trembling ceased and she was eager to get going. Gregg sensed the change in her and began walking along the rough trail between the cliffs.

Marcia glanced back, but she could not see the entrance to the cave. Gregg had certainly chosen the right place for them to hide out. Unless someone knew of the cave, it would be difficult to find, except perhaps by chance.

They walked in silence, too busy concentrating on the trail to talk. Somehow conversation did not seem important. Marcia could sense that Gregg felt that way, too.

As they continued along the path, the sound of the angry sea grew louder and more forceful. A few gulls cried in the misty air, their voices all but drowned out by the crash of the surf.

They had been on the trail about fifteen minutes when Gregg motioned for her to follow as he veered to the right. This new pathway was less worn and traveled, and Marcia had to watch her footing among the loose rocks that were strewn about.

It was a relief to her when they were suddenly on level ground once more. They had emerged by the long hedge that bracketed the garden. Ahead of them stood Windcliff, proud and remote, as though the house itself rejected what was going on within its walls.

"Looks as if we're in luck," Gregg said. "They're still sleeping. I don't see any lights. But maybe you'd better stay here where it's safe, Marcia. It could be a trap. They might be waiting for us with the lights off."

"No way," Marcia said. "If you're going back in the house, so am I. There's safety in numbers."

Gregg looked at her with a trace of humor in his eyes. "There's a lot of stubbornness in you, Marcia Carpenter."

"Let's just say I can be very tenacious when I want to."

The trace of humor spread to Gregg's lips and he smiled, showing his even teeth.

"I'm glad you're on my side. Are you ready to continue?"

"How far is the kitchen door?"

Gregg lifted his arm and pointed beyond the hedge. "Over there. The whole area is overgrown with ivy. If you didn't know it was there, you'd never find it."

"Are there any secrets to Windcliff that you don't know about?" Marcia asked in a mock serious voice.

"You forget I've had twenty-three years to learn all about this island."

To Marcia that was a long time. "In all those years, have you ever grown tired of the island and wished you were somewhere else?"

Gregg looked at her with astounded eyes. It was clear to Marcia that the thought had never crossed his mind.

"Windcliff is my home. I never tire of the island. The sea is constantly changing and the place suits me. I wouldn't live anywhere else."

"I know what you mean. There is something about the place that gets to you. It has to me."

Gregg's eyes glowed with a warmth that made Marcia temporarily forget the chill of the morning.

"I'm glad you feel that way. I'd hoped that you would like Teal Island."

"Does my liking the island really matter that much to you?"

"More than you know," Gregg said and then turned. "We'd better get going."

Marcia followed Gregg, thinking over what he had just said. Why did it mean so much to him that she liked Teal Island? After all, when this was all over, she would be returning to Penwick.

They hurried through the garden, and the house

appeared to draw nearer to them. At last they found themselves near the French doors leading off the study. Now they cautiously moved from window to window. Above them hung the balcony from which they had made their escape the night before.

They left the garden behind them. And Marcia felt the damp leaves of the ivy brush her face as they made their way toward the kitchen. Coming to an area that was particularly overgrown, Gregg caught her arm.

"We're there," he said.

Marcia looked around, but she could see nothing but vines and dense leaves. Then Gregg knelt and parted the vines so that a window could be seen. This was a window to the cellar.

"Let's pray that it isn't locked," Gregg said as he applied pressure to the window.

For a moment it appeared that Gregg's prayer wouldn't be answered. Then the window opened. Gregg slipped through the opening and Marcia heard him moving about below.

"It's all right. Just a slight drop. Nothing like climbing down the balcony."

Marcia squirmed her way through the dense growth of ivy and slipped feet first into the cellar. She felt Gregg's strong hands on her waist as he broke her fall.

The cellar was musty and dark, but Marcia found that once her eyes became accustomed to the dimness, she could see fairly well. It was a vast, sprawling room like all of the other rooms at Windcliff.

Along one wall was a wine rack with the rows of tilted bottles marked by age. The rack was constructed so that there was a narrow space between it and the wall. The temperature in the cellar was chilly, perhaps favorable for the wines but not for Marcia's mood. She wondered if she would ever be warm again.

Gregg had set about exploring the wide room. Old discarded furniture was stacked in one corner in a haphazard pile. Above the furniture and extending along the wall were shelves of canned goods.

"Maggie Holt, our housekeeper, wanted to be prepared for every emergency," Gregg said with a faint, ironic chuckle. "Whether it be fair or foul weather."

Marcia could see that if Windcliff ever lost contact with the mainland, its occupants need not worry about going hungry.

Moving past the furniture and the groaning shelves of canned goods, they came to a closed door.

"I have a hunch this is where they stored their stuff," Gregg said as he reached for the doorknob.

Slowly, the door creaked open. Striking a match, Gregg held it aloft as he peered into the room.

Marcia did not want to see what was inside. The whole idea of drugs was repulsive to her. She backed away from Gregg, wishing that they were out of this dreary place.

She was not aware of where she was going until she felt the movement behind her and heard the smash of a lamp as it toppled from the stack of furniture to the concrete floor.

The noise was like an explosion. Gregg shut the door and whirled to face Marcia. "I'm sorry. I wasn't looking," she managed to say.

At that moment there were footsteps overhead and the door to the cellar opened.

Gregg grabbed Marcia by the arm as he frantically looked for a hiding place. "There," he whispered, "behind the wine rack. Hurry."

They raced across the room and squeezed themselves into the narrow opening between the wall and the rack. None too soon. The overhead light was switched on and someone came down the stairs. By the glare of the light, Marcia could see that whoever it was held a gun in his hand.

CHAPTER THIRTEEN

As the footsteps descended the stairs, Marcia and Gregg braced themselves against the wall behind the wine rack. Marcia was afraid to breathe lest she be heard in that vast, quiet cellar.

"What's going on, Brock?" came a voice as another person joined the man who was descending the stairs.

It was Joe's voice and he was speaking to Brock, who must have been the first one to hear the noise of the lamp breaking.

"I thought I heard a noise down here. Evie and I were having coffee when I heard something smash."

Marcia inwardly died a thousand deaths thinking of how clumsy she had been. She and Gregg had come this far without being discovered and now, because of her actions, they stood a good chance of having Brock find them. Marcia glanced at Gregg, but his face was stoic. Only his eyes were alert, watchful.

Brock and Joe were nearing the bottom of the stairs. The area between the wine rack and the wall was in shadows, but if the two men decided to search the cellar, she and Gregg would easily be detected.

"You don't suppose it could be that Carpenter girl and young Spaniard?" Joe said.

Brock's voice was cold. "From what you told me, the boat they were on sank."

"That's right. I found some pieces of it washed

ashore. They won't be bothering us again. You don't think I would lie to you."

Brock snorted, "You know you'd be sorry if you did. But there is always the possibility that they escaped and swam ashore."

"I never thought of that," Joe said.

"Well, start thinking. If those two get to the police before we make contact with Racon, we'll be in big trouble. You want to serve more time in the slammer?"

Apparently, that remark didn't set too well with Joe. "If I go, so do you and Evie. Don't forget that, Mr. Braintrust."

Brock's voice changed its tone with his next words. He was obviously going to placate Joe. "Take it easy. We'll be out of this place soon. All we're waiting for is that signal from Penwick from Racon. Then we can kiss Teal Island good-bye."

"The sooner the better. When I get my share of this, it's off to California for me."

"In the meantime, let's find out what caused that racket down here," Brock said.

Marcia saw that Brock and Joe were slowly moving toward the stack of furniture. Her attention was suddenly shifted from them to the far corner where the lamp lay shattered. There was a scurrying sound from the pile of furniture, and a rat moved quickly out of the rubble of broken tables and chairs and darted across the room.

"There's your ghost," Joe said in a jeering tone. "Just a rat. Probably has a nest in that pile of junk."

Brock appeared to be satisfied with that explanation.

Marcia inwardly sighed with relief. Then her eyes moved to the open window through which Gregg and she had gained access to the cellar. What if Brock or Joe noticed the window? Would they have remembered that it had been shut before? Marcia turned to look at Gregg, who had been staring at the window also. His eyes shifted and met hers. There was no need for words. She could read what lay in their depths. He was worried, too.

"Better check on the stuff," Brock said as he scuffed along the rough concrete floor.

The door to the storage room was opened as Joe and Brock made a quick check inside.

Marcia heard Brock's sardonic laugh. "You are looking at about two hundred thousand dollars, my friend. How does that make you feel?"

"Great. Just great. Only, I'll be glad when this whole caper is finished. What's keeping Racon, I wonder?"

Brock shut the door with a bang. "I don't know. He was supposed to contact us last night."

"You don't suppose something's happened to him."

"Like what?"

"Like the police, for one thing."

Brock said, "Racon's too smart to fall into the hands of the authorities. Besides, the police in a hick town like Penwick would be like nothing to him. They couldn't give Racon any trouble."

Marcia had to clench her fists to keep from moving out from behind the rack. Even if Penwick was a small town, she didn't like the idea of someone running it down. Gregg sensed her feelings and reached out and put a restraining hand on her arm.

"Guess we'd better get back upstairs. Things look all right down here," Brock said. "You get back to the boat. Don't leave it unguarded for a minute."

Joe mumbled something as the two men went up the stairs. When they reached the top, the cellar was plunged once more into semi-darkness.

"Whew! That was too close for comfort," Gregg said.

"For a while there I thought for sure they'd notice the open window," Marcia said as she and Gregg moved out from behind the wine rack.

"That was dumb of me not to close it. But at least we know for certain why they are here and when they'll be leaving."

"Apparently, they can't do a thing until they get some signal from Racon."

"He must be in Penwick waiting for the right opportunity to get word to them. If there was only some way we could notify the authorities."

Marcia sighed. "Well, their boat is out. You heard what Brock told Joe about watching it. And it's a sure thing we can't swim to Penwick. What do we do now, Gregg?"

Gregg ran a hand through his dark hair. "All I can think of is getting back to the cave. We'd be a lot safer there than here. And maybe we can come up with some plan."

The thought of leaving the cellar was one that appealed to Marcia. After seeing that rat running across the floor she was uneasy about remaining here. What Windcliff needed was a good enterprising cat.

"I'll give you a boost to the window. Do you think you can manage from there?"

"No problem," Marcia said. "Just get me up there and I'll do the rest."

Gregg put his strong hands about her waist and effortlessly lifted Marcia from the floor until she was in line with the open window. Thrusting her arms through the small opening, Marcia quickly wriggled her way through the space. She got to her feet and waited until Gregg emerged a few seconds later.

She glanced down at her dress, which was streaked

with dust, and saw there was a small tear in the hemline. She figured her hair was a mess, but this was no time to worry about that.

"We'll have to be more careful going back to the cave," Gregg said. "Brock isn't completely convinced that we went down with the ship."

"Where do you suppose Evie was during that episode in the cellar?"

"Let's hope that she was taking Dad something to eat."

Suddenly the image of Joshia Spaniard flashed through Marcia's mind. She couldn't help feeling sorry for the old man lying helpless upstairs. She had to think as Gregg did that Brock would be humanitarian enough not to harm him. Otherwise she might break down and cry. Marcia was not the type to weep easily. Tears did come whenever something touched her heart, though. She bit her lips and firmly blinked the wetness from her eyes.

"Are you all right, sweetheart?" Gregg asked.

"Sure. It must have been the dust in the cellar," Marcia replied.

Gregg suddenly reached for her and tenderly held her. Marcia leaned her head against his strong chest just for a moment for the reassurance he offered.

"I'm all right, Gregg. Hadn't we better get back to the cave? I'm getting hungry. And maybe we can think better on a full stomach."

"Good for you. We'll beat Brock at his own game yet."

By now the sun had burned through the fog and it shone with a dazzling brilliance. Across the bay Marcia could see Penwick as the fog lifted. Last night's rain had left the flowers and the leaves on the trees glistening with gleaming droplets of water.

They hurried along the side of the house keeping as

low a profile as they were able to. When they came to the garden, Gregg headed toward the high shrubbery which formed a natural boundary for the garden. Here they walked in a crouched position, glancing back every now and then to make certain they had not been seen.

Suddenly Gregg stopped. He motioned Marcia behind a tree and she followed him nervously.

From where they stood they could see the walk that led to the servants' quarters. Evie was coming toward them. She seemed preoccupied as she carried a picnic hamper over her arm. Deep in thought, Evie passed no more than a few feet from their place of concealment. Just beyond the tree, Evie paused as though she were conscious of something. She turned and glanced back over the trail. Gregg and Marcia crouched, letting the shrubbery conceal them even more. Evie shrugged and then continued on her way to the house.

When they were sure Evie had gone into the house, Gregg and Marcia stepped out from behind the tree.

"That was close," Marcia said with a sigh of relief. "Where do you suppose she was going? And with a picnic hamper."

"I seriously doubt that she was coming from a clambake," Gregg said with a wry smile. "That looked more like Evie was taking food to someone."

Marcia glanced at the servants' cottage. "Do you think they've got someone locked in the servants' quarters?"

"Unless I miss my guess, Carl and Maggie are in there. That's the only logical place they could be. After Brock took over the house, he and Joe must have surprised the Holts and locked them up in the cottage."

"Then Evie must have been taking food to them in that hamper," Marcia said.

"At least they aren't starving to death."

Marcia remembered the nurse's cap she had found. The one that had gotten her locked in her room.

"If the Holts are in there, then maybe your father's nurse is with them. That's where I found her cap."

"You're probably right. Nurse Daniels was supposed to go to the mainland and see about a replacement. Since she wasn't a local nurse, nobody has missed her at Penwick."

Gregg made a fist and struck his open palm with it in anger. "I feel so helpless. It's so unbelievable that strangers can just walk in and take over the way Brock and Joe and Evie did."

There was nothing Marcia could say since she knew how Gregg felt. One minute you were safe and secure in your home, and the next a prisoner, helpless, at the mercy of your captors. And the frightening thing was that it could happen to anybody.

"Are you game to go check the servants' cottage? Or would you rather go back to the hideout and eat something?"

"Food can wait," she said. "I'm just as curious as you are about that cottage. Maybe there will be some way we can help the Holts and Nurse Daniels."

"Remind me when this is all over to tell you that I think you're great," Gregg said and smiled warmly at her.

"That's a deal. And I must remind you that I have a very good memory."

With that said, they both moved once again along the pathway to the servants' cottage. The ever-present wind which had subsided somewhat sprang up again, whipping Marcia's dress against her legs. If it weren't for the warm rays of the sun, she would have been cold even within the confines of her sweater.

When they arrived at the small house, Gregg tried

the door, but it was securely locked. There was no way they could see in through the boarded-up windows, but they moved from window to window in the vain hope that one of them might accidentally give them access to the cottage.

"It's no use," Gregg finally said. "Brock has the place locked up tighter than a drum. If the Holts and Nurse Daniels are in there, they are probably bound and gagged."

"This may sound like a foolish question, but isn't there a key someplace in the house that would unlock the door?"

"They put a padlock on it. And probably only Brock or Evie have a key," Gregg said with disappointment.

It was hard for them to leave the cottage, knowing that there might possibly be hostages inside, but they were in ever-present danger staying outdoors.

Together they turned and started back to the path which led to the cave. As they walked along, taking care to stay as close to the hedge as possible, Marcia once again got the feeling that eyes were following their every movement.

"Gregg, ever since I've come here I've had this feeling that someone was watching me."

"It's probably just your nerves. Can't say I blame you for feeling that way what with everything that's happened to you since you arrived."

They had come to the cliffs and, below, the gray water roared against the slick black rocks. From where they stood they could see down the beach to the boathouse. Holding Marcia's hand tightly in his, Gregg started down the steep pathway. As they neared a section of the cliff where they could observe the beach without being seen, Gregg suddenly stopped.

To their right they saw Brock and Joe hunched over

something on the ground. Their voices carried in the wind.

"What's so interesting about a blanket?" Joe asked in his hoarse voice.

"Haven't you seen this blanket before?"

"It's just a blanket. Why all the fuss?"

Marcia swallowed. That had been careless of her—to have thrown the blanket away last night when she and Gregg were running on the beach.

"This blanket was in the boathouse. I remember seeing it on a shelf there."

"So?" Joe asked.

"So that means that somebody took it from the boathouse. Probably to dry off after they had been in the water."

Joe stood up abruptly. "You aren't saying that Spaniard and the Carpenter dame didn't drown last night?"

"That's exactly what I am saying. They're alive and somewhere on the island."

Gregg and Marcia didn't wait to hear any more. They headed down the pathway, away from Brock and Joe, as fast as they could. It was to their advantage that Gregg knew the island so well. Even at that it seemed hours to Marcia before they arrived at the concealed entrance to the hideout. Gregg motioned Marcia into the passageway and was right behind her as she stumbled along the dark corridor.

When they came at last to the end of the tunnel, Marcia leaned against the rough stone wall while Gregg struck a match to the lantern. Her heart was beating so wildly it was like a trip-hammer in her ears.

Gregg moved toward Marcia and took her hand, leading her to a chair. "Our one advantage is gone. They know we're alive now."

CHAPTER FOURTEEN

"But they'll never find us here," Marcia said in an attempt to be optimistic. "So we have at least that going for us."

Gregg was thoughtful as he moved across the room to the fireplace. He didn't speak for a few minutes so Marcia moved to his side.

"You have every right to be angry with me," she said. "That was inexcusable, leaving the blanket behind."

"You had no way of knowing that it would be found or that Brock had been aware of it in the boathouse. It's just one of those things. Don't blame yourself."

Marcia felt better and she knew that Gregg had meant what he said. Sudden hunger pangs forced her to turn her attention to the far wall where the canned goods were stored. She walked over and eyed the well-stocked shelves. Taking down a small canned ham, she began opening it.

"Do you enjoy your work at Penwick?" Gregg said as he watched her opening the can.

"Very much. Adam's clients have all been very nice to me. And I feel that I help them in my way. So that is satisfying to me."

"Does Adam have many clients?"

"I'm afraid if he had to depend on the citizens of Penwick to support him, he would be in a bad way. Fortunately, he handles a lot of clients from out of town. They must pay him very well. He has a beautiful and expensive home on the outskirts of town."

Gregg walked over to where Marcia was working and began setting the table. They spoke of their high school days and the good times they had had in school. Even though there was a difference in their ages, Marcia still knew most of Gregg's school chums. They laughed and joked with abandon as they ate ham on stale crackers. Although Gregg had the advantages of wealth, he was in no way condescending or a snob. Marcia felt at ease with him.

"Tell me about your childhood. I want to know all about you," Gregg said, reaching for another slice of ham.

Marcia told him about her father as best she could recall. How he had made a good living from the sea. Her eyes moistened when she spoke of his accident, and Gregg reached out and tenderly touched her hand.

"You've had it rough, haven't you?" Gregg said.

Marcia blinked away the tears. "Oh, no. My mother was sweet and loving. She was a very strong person. Even though we didn't have a lot of money, her love made up for any lack of material things."

"She sounds like a wonderful person," Gregg said.

Marcia remembered what she had been told about Gregg's mother. How she had deserted him when he was young. Gregg began to talk about her and the artist who had come to paint her portrait.

"He was quite a romantic figure, they say. My mother was swept off her feet by his charm. She had never cared for life on the island and I'm certain that she liked my father a great deal but never loved him.

She was quite a few years younger than he. Dad saw what was happening but didn't do anything about it. He loved my mother very much and wouldn't stand in the way of her happiness. She ran away with the artist when the portrait was finished, and Dad divorced her."

"Did you ever hear from her? Weren't there any letters?"

"Only one. It was written just before the day of the accident. She sent her love."

Marcia waited, watching the agony etch itself on Gregg's face.

"Her second husband was a reckless driver and he drank too much. One afternoon, after he had been drinking, they went for a drive. The car swerved off the road, and he overcorrected and the car rolled over. They were both instantly killed."

Gregg's face was drawn with lines. Then they slowly vanished as he went on. "Dad became both mother and father to me. But he was strict and made certain that I didn't turn out to be a spoiled brat."

"I would say he succeeded admirably," Marcia said, gazing into Gregg's dark eyes.

"Thanks. What I am today I owe to Joshia Spaniard. He did everything for me when I was growing up. Now that he's bedridden, it's my turn to take care of him."

After that they spoke no more of their childhood and their parents. Marcia felt that she had gotten to know Gregg almost as though she had grown up with him. There were no lapses that she couldn't account for. She realized how much she loved Gregg, but she tried to put this out of her mind. She couldn't be certain that what she felt was love was not just overwhelming compassion.

After an hour Gregg had become restless. He

prowled the cave like a caged animal. Then he said, "Marcia, I'm going back to the house."

"What? You can't be serious."

"Dead serious. If I can find some way to repair the telephone lines, I could slip inside the house and call for help."

Marcia felt a cold chill course through her body. "You could be walking into a trap."

"I could be. But my hunch is that Brock and Joe wouldn't think I had the nerve to come back to the house. They might be scouting the island trying to find this place."

"Then I want to go with you," Marcia said.

"Not this time. Now that they found the blanket, they'll be on their guard. I want you to stay here where you will be safe."

Marcia would have spoken up, but she saw the determined look in Gregg's face and she knew her protesting wouldn't have done her any good.

Before Gregg left, he took her in his arms and she leaned her head against a broad shoulder. When, she thought, will I be seeing him again?

"Try to be careful," she murmured.

"I'll be back as soon as I can." With that Gregg was gone, lost in the dark, shadowy tunnel.

For a moment Marcia fought the desire to follow him, whether he liked it or not. Then she sighed. Gregg knew the island like the back of his hand. She would only slow him up if she went along. And if he got the telephone wires repaired, it wouldn't be long until help came.

Now that she was alone, she glanced around the hideout for something to occupy her time until he returned. With Gregg gone, the black shadows seemed to creep toward her.

She tossed her head and said aloud, "Don't let this

place get the best of you, girl. Gregg will be back."

That helped. Marcia walked over to the shelves that Gregg must have built, bringing the lumber over from Windcliff. She ran her hand over them, imagining how he must have toiled getting them all in place. He was so wonderful, so capable.

She found a paperback novel. It was a Western, not the kind of book she normally read, but she figured it would take her mind off her situation. Drawing a chair up near the lantern, she sat with her legs curled beneath her as she became engrossed in life in the far West.

Halfway through the book, she paused, wondering what time it was. If only Gregg had thought about putting a clock in the hideout when he had found it. Marcia figured that at least two hours had elapsed since Gregg had gone to Windcliff. Had something happened to him? What if Brock or—worse yet—Joe had found him? Somehow she felt that Joe was more capable of violence than Brock.

"Don't think about that. Think positive," she said. Getting up, she went to the table and picked up a cracker. She took one bite and tasted its staleness, then tossed it into the fireplace.

She felt restless, uneasy. She began to pace the room, wishing that she had a cup of coffee. Marcia knew better than to start a fire in the fireplace now. Even the faintest trickle of smoke would be enough to give her presence away.

With a deep sigh, Marcia returned to her book. She tried to concentrate on the story, but she found herself rereading sentence after sentence and then not understanding what she had just read. Finally, in exasperation, she tossed the book aside and sat huddled in the chair.

She thought about her apartment back in Penwick. Fortunately, she had given all the plants inside a good healthy watering before she left. She wondered when she would see it again. Suddenly she missed the security and comfort of the small, cozy apartment. Marcia snuggled inside the warmth of the sweater. The cave was cold and damp.

Then Marcia saw Gregg's sleeping bag rolled up in the corner. What a ninny she was. Here Gregg was outside trying his best to get them out of this mess and all she could do was feel sorry for herself.

She decided to explore the cave. This would give her something to do. Taking the lantern, she began walking through the wide, shadowy room. As she approached the far wall, she saw another passageway. It looked high enough so that she would not have to stoop in order to walk through it. Marcia wondered where it led or if it ended a short distance from the main room.

Curiosity beckoned to her and she entered the passageway. Her footsteps echoed dully in the hollow depths of the tunnel. Once a soft silken something touched her forehead and she quickly brushed the spider web away.

As she slowly moved through the tunnel, she wondered if there might be rats running loose. She vividly recollected the episode in the cellar, where the rat had kept them from being discovered by Brock and Joe. The glow from the lantern did not give out much light, so it was impossible for her to see more than a short distance ahead.

There was little air in the passageway and what air there was was stale. It reminded Marcia of the attic in the house where she and her mother had lived. The attic had been closed for years and she had wandered in one rainy afternoon. She remembered that the door had closed on her and she had experienced a feeling of panic until she had gotten out of the place.

Lost in thought, Marcia was not looking down until her foot struck a small stone. It skittered, then fell with an echoing clamor into hollow space. Marcia's instincts told her to freeze. She looked down at where she was about to step, seeing a yawning, deadly pit that she might have fallen into.

She moved slowly backward as if the dark shaft behind her possessed some magnetism that could draw her into its depths. Holding the lantern high over her head she pivoted and ran back to the safety of the cave's main room.

Once she was out of the tunnel, she shuddered, thinking how close she had come to falling into the pit. She could have been killed or been so badly hurt she couldn't have climbed out.

What was keeping Gregg? Why hadn't he returned? Had something happened to him? It was useless to try not to worry. The plain truth was that she was scared and Gregg hadn't returned. She paced back and forth across the expanse of the hideout, thinking.

She had promised Gregg that she would stay here, but somehow she had the feeling that his plans had gone wrong. Maybe, if she was careful, she could leave the cave and go in search of him. If he was all right, the most that would happen would be that he would be angry. And if he were hurt or in trouble, she might be able to help him.

Marcia put out the light in the lantern. She felt her way to the entrance of the tunnel. By now she had become almost familiar with its twists and turns. Even though she was walking in darkness, she made rapid progress. Before long, she saw daylight outside and she quickened her steps.

Emerging from the darkness of the tunnel, she blinked in the bright sunlight. The sky was a light blue with a few cotton balls of clouds. She breathed deeply, glad to be free of the dank cave and its stuffy air. If her stay outside was only to be temporary, she meant to get as much out of it as possible. Below her the sea was like a cobalt carpet dotted with whitecaps. At any other time it would have been an impressive sight.

She moved along the trail that led to higher ground, being careful not to let herself make too good a target.

The wind was not as intense as it had been earlier and she heard no sound except an occasional seagull as it swooped overhead.

She had no idea where to begin to search for Gregg. He had said that he was going to check the telephone line to see if he could repair the slashed wires. That meant he had to be somewhere in the vicinity of Windcliff. Probably at the rear of the house. So Marcia turned off the trail and headed toward the garden. Now and then she paused to look and listen. And she once again felt those unseen eyes watching her. Where was this watcher of Windcliff, and who was he?

Uneasily Marcia moved toward the rear of the house. In the distance, she could see the small cottage where the Holts and Nurse Daniels were held captive. If Gregg and she could only set them free, surely all of them would be able to overpower Brock and Joe. Or would they? Even with that extra help, they wouldn't be much good against the guns that the intruders had.

The pathway began to smooth out and Marcia found herself on level land once more. Windcliff was to her left and she stood midway between the stately mansion and the servants' quarters. Not far ahead was the hedge which encircled the rear of the house. Marcia hurried to the safety of a twisted tree where she could survey the grounds.

She saw Gregg at the same time he saw her. He was half concealed in the dense growth of ivy, and if she hadn't been looking for him, she might have missed him.

Seeing her Gregg began to wave frantically with his hand and pointed to her left. Marcia quickly glanced in the direction Gregg was pointing. Joe was walking along the pathway headed toward her.

Marcia left the safety of the tree and headed in another direction from Joe. She hurried down the rock-strewn trail as fast as she dared. She prayed that she had been quick enough, that Gregg's warning had come in time. She dared not stop and glance over her shoulder. There wasn't time to see if she was being pursued.

Soon Marcia realized that she was just a short distance from the hideout. Her lungs felt as though they would burst and the beat of her heart throbbed in her ears.

When she ran into the entrance of the cave, she collapsed in a heap on the hard, rocky floor of the tunnel.

CHAPTER FIFTEEN

After lying on the chilly floor of the tunnel for a few minutes, Marcia found that her breathing slowly became normal. She sat up. The near encounter with Joe had been too close for comfort. If Gregg hadn't warned her, she would have practically walked into the waiting arms of Joe.

She suddenly remembered what Brock had said about Joe standing guard over the boat. But that had been before the two of them had discovered the blanket she had cast off. How could she have been so careless in tossing it aside?

The dampness of the tunnel floor began to seep into her clothing, and she quickly got to her feet. Realizing how near she still was to the entrance, she hurried into the darkness until she was once more in the hideout.

Fumbling in the dark, she found the box of matches and struck one, touching its small flame to the wick of the lantern. The lantern's welcome glow swept the shadows back against the rocky edges of the walls.

Marcia found that she was hungry after all the exercise she had just had. She opened a tin of cookies and grabbed a handful.

She longed for the warmth of a fire in the fireplace but again she knew better than to light one. Slipping into a chair, she sat nibbling on the cookies trying to decide what she should do next.

Gregg was all right. At least she had found that much out by her foray into the outside world. She hoped he wouldn't be angry at her for leaving the cave. It had been an unwise thing to do, especially after he had told her to stay put. But at least she knew for certain that he was unharmed. That in itself was worth the near confrontation with Joe.

Marcia wondered if Gregg had been successful in repairing the damaged telephone line. If he had, then maybe this nightmare would soon be over. Then she could return to Penwick, her apartment, and her job. If Clarita Hooper only knew what she had been going through. This was one time Marcia had the edge on the woman. Although she would have given anything not to be going through this experience.

And what of Adam Long? She wondered how he was faring in New York. Was his trip successful? If he had only known what danger he had placed her in by sending her to Teal Island. Yet if she hadn't come, she never would have really met Gregg. They never, in all probability, would have become so close.

Thinking of Gregg made the whole unpleasant experience bearable. What if he had gone away to Boston, as planned, and she had been left at the mercy of Brock Janis? Marcia shivered. That was too horrible to contemplate. She doubted that she would have had the nerve to climb down from the balcony if Gregg hadn't been waiting below in case she slipped.

Marcia took a bite from a cookie as she mentally saw Joshia's wan face lying on the stark white pillow of his bed. He was so helpless, so unable to defend himself. At least Brock had shown some degree of humanity in bringing Evie along to care for the old man. Though Evie appeared to be as hard as nails, Marcia felt that it was just a cover-up.

If she scraped those layers of makeup off, she would be a very pretty girl. No doubt Evie only made herself up because Brock liked her that way. Evie had had a hard life bouncing around the country from job to job, so it was little wonder that she grabbed hold of Brock when he gave her a little attention. Somehow Marcia had the feeling that as soon as this job was over and Brock had his money, he would ditch Evie.

Brock was not the sort of man who could be tied down to one woman. She remembered how he had looked at her the afternoon she had arrived at Teal Island. Evie had seen that look, too, and had rushed in to protect her property. Not that Evie had anything to worry about. Brock was just not her type. And Marcia very much doubted that he was Evie's, for that matter. It was a one-sided romance and when Evie came to her senses, she would see just what sort of man Brock Janis really was.

Marcia finished the cookie and stared at the ashes in the fireplace. For a moment she wished that Brock would contact Racon and leave the island. Then she realized what that would mean. All the nightmares and crime that would follow after he delivered the drugs. She knew she wouldn't be able to rest knowing that she and Gregg might have been able to prevent that delivery. But what could they do against guns?

Thoughts swirled around in Marcia's head, bringing with them a feeling of lethargy. She was suddenly very tired. Getting up from the chair, she unrolled her sleeping bag and stretched out. Futility took its toll and she closed her eyes and slept.

It was not a peaceful sleep, for in her dreams she found herself back at Windcliff once again. Only, this time there were no doors on any of the rooms. She ran feverishly from room to room, searching for someone or something. All the rooms were empty, and dust had collected on the floors and draperies. The windows were broken and the house looked as though it had not been lived in for years.

She cried out Gregg's name, her voice echoing throughout the empty, deserted house. Then she ran up the circular staircase that wobbled beneath her as though it would come crashing down at any minute. When she got to the second floor, she raced breathlessly to the hallway. There at the end of the hallway stood a wraithlike figure. It began to advance toward her, and as it drew nearer she saw that it was Joshia Spaniard.

He raised a warning hand and said, "Danger! Danger!"

Marcia awoke in a cold sweat. She sat up, shaking her head to clear it of the dream. It had been so vivid that when she glanced around, she almost expected to find herself at Windcliff.

"It was only a dream," she said aloud, needing the comfort of hearing a human voice even if it was only her own.

She wondered how long she had slept or, for that matter, dreamed. She had read somewhere that dreams take place usually in a matter of minutes so she had not really slept very long.

What was keeping Gregg? Surely by this time he had been able to repair the telephone wires. If he had been successful, then there was the matter of entering the house without being seen. That would be the tricky part. Suppose he had been able to get inside, and Brock or Joe had caught him. She mustn't think of that. Gregg was too cautious to allow himself to be captured. But why didn't he come back?

Marcia got up from the sleeping bag and rolled it

back into a tight bundle. She secretly prayed that she wouldn't have to use it again, that she would not have to spend another night in the hideout. Without the warmth of the fireplace, the cave was dank and chilly and anything but cheerful.

In a small brown case with a broken zipper she found a brush and a mirror. She was almost afraid to glance into the mirror for fear of how she would look. But outside of a smudge here and there, her face was all right. But her hair was a mass of snarls and tangles. Propping the mirror on the table, Marcia sat down and began unsnarling her hair. The brush had a soothing effect on her, and she wanted to appear reasonably presentable when Gregg came back.

After she had given her hair the necessary brush strokes, she filled a shallow pan with water and luckily found a bar of soap. She washed her face in the cold water, then found a clean dish towel to dry herself. Now that she had brushed her hair and cleansed her face, she felt better.

Marcia glanced around at the cave and suddenly she knew that she just couldn't stay there any longer. She had been careless the last time, but now she would watch out for danger. And besides, she tried to reassure herself, she wouldn't venture too far from the hideout.

Snuffing out the lantern, she hurried through the tunnel until she emerged into the diffused sunlight. She cautiously picked her way along the path, pausing now and then to listen for any unfamiliar sound. The wind whipped along the pathway, but Marcia had become so accustomed to it that she barely felt its sting.

She had only planned on going a short distance, but the farther she ventured from the cave, the more the idea of returning to that dismal place lost its appeal. When she came to where the pathway branched off to

the trail leading to Windcliff, she hesitated. Marcia
debated whether or not to continue. Then, resolutely,
her stubborn nature came to the fore. She recalled
what her father had told her when she had become
indecisive as a little girl. "Chart your course, child.
Keep your eye on the horizon and don't look back."

Marcia hurried off the pathway and headed up the
face of the cliff with determined strides. The wind was
refreshing after she had been cooped up in the hideout.
High in the sky, gulls wheeled looking like gray vees
against the overcast blueness. She was uncaring but
mindful of the eyes that followed her as she climbed
the rugged trail. Below her the restless waves roared
like a living entity. Marcia had lost her fear of them.
She had been tossed into their watery depths, yet she
had survived.

Somehow she had overcome her childhood fear, and
that knowledge was like a heavy weight that had been
lifted from her shoulders. If for no other reason than
that, Teal Island had been good for her.

Once on the higher ground, Marcia paused after she
had taken refuge behind a thick clump of bushes.
From here she could see without being seen. Windcliff
was to her left, sprawling against the horizon with a
stark magnificence. The lower section of the house
was hidden from her view by the hedge. It was
impossible for her to see Gregg from the bushes.

Marcia slowly stood up on her toes. Now she could
see over the hedge and into the garden, and beyond the
garden. Her eyes clung like a soft, leafy-green drapery.
She saw no sign of Gregg or any movement in the ivy.
He must have found the telephone wires and
reconnected them. He might at this very moment be
inside Windcliff making that urgent call.

She stepped out from behind her covering and then

leaped back as she heard a door slam. Someone was coming along the garden path. In the security of the bushes, she saw Brock walking purposefully toward the servants' quarters. Even though Marcia was protected from his view, she still felt a twinge of fear that trickled down her spine.

As Brock neared her hiding place, he paused as though he were aware of someone watching him. He turned his head in her direction and she saw his cold blue eyes that reminded her of a serpent. Brock appeared to be satisfied that he wasn't being watched, then continued in the direction of the small cottage.

Her view was cut off by the hedge and a few scattered wind-battered trees. Marcia decided that she would follow Brock. That way, at least, she would know his whereabouts. Joe was probably down at the beach keeping watch over their boat, and Evie was no doubt still inside the house. If Brock opened the door to the servants' quarters, she might have the opportunity to see if the Holts and Nurse Daniels were inside.

With cautious steps, Marcia left the safety of the bushes and hurried to the hedge where she walked in a crouched position. She knew this was risky and she was tempted to turn around and go back to the safety of the hideout. Yet she felt compelled to continue on.

When she came to the end of the hedge, she peered around its thorny growth. There was no sign of Brock. He must be in the cottage for whatever purpose he had for going there. Between where the hedge ended and the cottage stood, there were only scattered patches of shrubbery and a few twisted trees. She would have to make a run for it in order to reach the safety of a tree.

Once she was safely behind the trunk of a tree, she peered out at the cottage. She did not see Brock anywhere. He must have already gone inside the house. Marcia thought that he must have been in a great hurry to have traveled that distance in such a short span of time.

She moved from tree to tree fully aware that she could be seen as she dashed across the open expanse of land. Yet there was no way she could avoid that. She hoped that Brock was so intent on the prisoners at the cottage that he wouldn't expect to be followed.

The nearer she came to the servants' quarters, the more uneasy she became. It was a long way back to Gregg's hideout, and the farther she roamed, the more she put herself in jeopardy.

Now she had arrived close enough to the cottage so that she could clearly view the front door. It stood open slightly so she knew that Brock had gone in. If she could only get a glimpse of the inside to make certain that its occupants were all right.

She left the sanctuary of the tree she had been hiding behind and carefully inched her way to the cottage. She glanced around, but there was no one to be seen. If it became necessary for her to make a break for it, she oriented herself in the direction she would have to take.

Now her attention was focused on the open door. She listened, straining her ears for a sound from the inside of the cottage. All was quiet. She stepped on a dead branch and the sound was like an explosion. Marcia held her breath, poised to bolt if she were discovered.

Since the noise had not attracted any attention from Brock, she moved nearer to the open door. Now she was close enough so that she could look inside. She squinted into the darkened interior, trying vainly to see either Brock or the other inhabitants. It was just too dark. Marcia moved even closer. She was unaware of everything but what she had come to find out.

She did not see the shadow that moved stealthily behind her, so quietly in that afternoon light. She did not see the arm that was raised until the hand clamped itself over her mouth.

Her head was forced back and she stared into the cold, deadly eyes of Brock Janis.

CHAPTER SIXTEEN

"So you weren't drowned after all," Brock said as he released his hold on Marcia's mouth, then held one of her arms in a viselike grip. "I thought as much when we found the blanket."

Marcia was so startled she could only stare into his cool eyes.

A mocking grin spread across Brock's lips.

"You fell into my trap nicely."

"What trap?" Marcia said.

"I saw you hiding in that clump of bushes. You thought I didn't see you. But I did. I left the cottage door open, just a crack, for you. And you fell for it."

"You knew all along that I would follow you."

"Of course. Curiosity caught the cat. Or in your case the kitten."

Marcia tried to break free from his grasp, but Brock was stronger than he looked.

"No use struggling. You might hurt yourself."

Brock's grip grew stronger and Marcia didn't like the ugly look in his eyes. This man was capable of great cruelty. So Marcia ceased struggling. If she caught him off guard, she might be able to make a break for it.

"That's better. You are being sensible now. You're much too pretty a kitten to be hurt."

Brock reached out and closed the door to the cottage with his free hand.

"What do you intend doing with me?" Marcia asked.

"I have plans," Brock said with a smirk. Marcia didn't like the way he said that or the diabolical gleam in his eye.

"You can't get away with this. I know all about the drugs hidden in the cellar. And we know that you mean to sell it to Racon."

Brock's hand tightened on her arm, and Marcia bit back tears of pain in her eyes.

"That's too bad. You really shouldn't have pried. It would have been safer for you not to have found out about the stuff."

"You wouldn't do anything to me."

Brock's lips twisted in a jeering grin. "There really isn't any choice, is there?"

"Gregg won't let you get away with it! He knows all about your plans!"

At the mention of Gregg's name, angry lines formed around Brock's eyes.

"He won't try anything. That is if he doesn't want you to get hurt. He'll come looking for you. I'm banking on that. But we'll be waiting for him."

Marcia realized what she had done by her impetuous move from the cave. She had not only put herself in jeopardy but Gregg was well. She decided to try a diversionary tactic.

"What's in the cottage that's so important to you? More stolen stuff?"

Brock glanced at the cottage door. "Just some unfortunate people who happened to be here at the wrong time."

"You mean the Holts and Nurse Daniels?"

"So you figured that out," he said.

"I thought you said the nurse had gone to the mainland. That her replacement would be coming soon."

Brock sighed impatiently. "A story for your benefit, Miss Carpenter. When you arrived unexpectedly, we had to come up with a convincing story. If it hadn't been for the storm, you would have returned to Penwick none the wiser. But the longer you remained, the deeper you became involved. When you found Nurse Daniels's cap, then we knew you couldn't be allowed to return to Penwick.

"You might have begun asking questions. You might even have gone to the police. We couldn't take any chances. Joe was all for getting rid of you, but Evie came to your rescue. I think it was more because she was against Joe than she was for you. Our mistake was thinking you would be safe locked in your room. We hadn't thought about the balcony or Gregg in the next room."

Apparently, Brock didn't know that Adam Long had informed her that the nurse was scheduled to leave. But this was not the time to mention that.

Instead, Marcia spoke as calmly as possible. "Then you found out how Gregg and I escaped."

"It was fairly obvious. Also, we knew you would try to use one of the boats. I had thought of that before, so I had Joe make certain they were not seaworthy."

"We could have drowned."

"I thought you had. Then when we found the blanket, I realized you had managed to swim ashore. We searched the island, but with no success. Just where did you hide, my little kitten?"

"You're so clever, you figure it out," Marcia couldn't help saying, realizing that she might incur Brock's wrath. If she got him angry enough, he might be caught off guard.

"It's not important," Brock said smugly. "What is important is that I have you."

Brock nudged her forward.

"Where are we going?" she asked.

"Back to the house. It will be easier to keep an eye on you there. Only, this time we won't make the mistake of leaving you alone."

Marcia staggered alongside Brock, who deliberately took long strides so that she had difficulty in keeping up with him. Her arm ached beneath the pressure of his fingers. She could only think of one thing, to escape from him before they reached the house.

When they were nearing the pathway that led to the beach, she pretended to turn her ankle. She dropped to the ground and Brock instinctively let go of her arm.

"I twisted my ankle. Can I rest a minute," she said, feigning a hurt tone.

Brock did not seem the least concerned about her, and he turned his back so that he was facing the house.

Seizing the opportunity, Marcia sprang to her feet and ran desperately toward the beach trail. She had gone only a short distance when she felt Brock's presence behind her. Marcia began to weave in her downward flight in a vain effort to keep Brock from grabbing her.

As she came to a jagged section of the cliffs, she suddenly was jerked to a standstill. The impact was so swift, her head snapped back. Brock's strong hands dug into her shoulders.

Below her, she saw a long drop to the jagged rocks. For a moment she had the paralyzing feeling that Brock was going to push her over the edge of the cliff. She gasped in terror.

"Are you afraid I might let you fall?" His voice was chilly. "It might make things a little easier,"

Marcia waited breathlessly, wondering whether Brock was going through with it.

Instead he laughed. "That would be too easy. Besides, I need you. Gregg will be easier to handle if you're left alive."

Once again Brock took one of her arms as they headed back in the direction of the house. Marcia felt defeated. She had tried to run away but had failed. Now Brock would be more watchful. Any further actions of hers would be suspect. She had to play along with him. Perhaps she would still come up with a plan of escape. Although that looked pretty hopeless at the present time.

When they got to the house, Brock shoved her through some open French doors. She found herself in the study.

"You were right," came Evie's hard voice. "They didn't drown. Where's Gregg?"

Brock shot Evie an angry look. "Don't worry, he'll be coming around. In the meantime, we'll keep an eye on Marcia."

Evie stood with her arms crossed and her feet planted firmly on the floor. She had really gone in heavily with the cosmetics today. Marcia thought she looked like a clown. Why did she go in for all that makeup? Why did she deliberately distort her natural good looks?

"Where did you find her?" Evie asked.

"You might say she found me. Or I let her think so anyway. She was snooping around the servants' quarters when I caught her."

Marcia said nothing. She only glared defiantly at Brock.

"Any coffee left?" Brock asked as Evie shut the French doors and locked them.

"In the kitchen. I'll get you a cup."

"Never mind," Brock said with a wave of his hand.
"I'll do it. You stay here and keep an eye on her. Only
this time do a good job."

Marcia couldn't help but notice the tilt of Evie's
eyebrow as Brock walked briskly out of the room.

"Sit down," Evie said roughly. "I don't want any
trouble out of you. You got me in enough as it is."

Marcia sat on one of the leather chairs. There was an
end table nearby with a book and a chewed-up pencil
next to a pad of paper. The book was a mystery that
had seen better days.

"So you managed to swim back to shore. Got to
hand it to you. You and Gregg don't give up easily."

"Why should we? After all, we didn't ask to be held
hostages."

Evie opened a pack of cigarettes and took one out.
She touched the end with the flame from her lighter.
Then she settled herself in a chair opposite Marcia.
Her back was to the French doors, while Marcia faced
the doors. If she tried to escape, she would have to go
past Evie.

"Why don't you just settle down and take it easy?"
Evie said. "At least until we're gone. Which shouldn't
be too much longer. It'll be easier on all of us."

"I don't want to make it easier on you. Just wait
until Gregg finds where I am."

Evie's face softened. A faint smile played on her lips.

"Kinda sweet on that guy, aren't you?"

Marcia tried to fight the warmth that spread across
her cheeks. Evie appeared to be enjoying her reaction.

"You can't fool me. Not that I blame you. Gregg's a
good-looking guy. It's only natural that the two of you
would get together."

Marcia changed the subject. "What will happen to

you after you leave the island?"

"Strictly a rose garden. I told you that Brock said we'd get married."

"How can you believe he'll do what he says? How do you know he's not just using you?"

Evie blew a cloud of smoke toward the high, vaulted ceiling.

"It won't work," she said with a wry smile. "I know what you're trying to do. Just chalk it up as one strike against you. It just so happens that I know Brock better than you do. He wouldn't dare dump me. Not with me knowing all I know."

Marcia wanted to keep Evie talking. Stall for time, she thought. Give Gregg a chance to find out where she was.

"Are you taking good care of Joshia? How is he feeling?"

What might have been called a look of compassion crossed Evie's heavily made-up face. "He's still the same. Only, I wish we'd get out of here so that a real nurse could look after him. The admiral's a sweet old guy and I wouldn't want anything to happen to him."

"Can I see him? What harm would it do?"

Evie shook her head. "Brock said you're to stay put. Besides, the admiral can't speak and you'd just upset him. There'll be plenty of time to see him after we're gone."

"You don't really mean that," Marcia said. "You know as well as I that Brock won't let any of us off this island alive."

For a moment there was a worried look in Evie's eyes.

"Come off it. Brock won't harm the old man. Or you, for that matter. It's not the way he does things. Murder isn't part of his business."

Marcia pressed on. She wanted to see Joshia. She had to be certain that he was unharmed.

"I know Joshia Spaniard can't speak. But couldn't I see him for just a moment? You can't be so hard that you wouldn't allow me to at least see for myself that he's all right."

Brock had come into the room as Marcia finished speaking. He took a sip of coffee, then said to Evie, "What's she going on about?"

Evie snuffed out her cigarette nervously in an ashtray. "She's got it in her head that we've done something with the admiral. She won't believe that I've given him nothing but tender loving care."

For an instant Brock looked at Marcia over the brim of his cup. Then he shrugged. "I see no reason why you can't take her up to his room. Only, watch her every move. All the doors are locked, but I don't want her trying to make a break for it."

"Whatever you say," Evie said as she got to her feet. "Come on, Marcia."

Marcia stood up and followed Evie out of the room, aware of Brock's cold eyes that followed her every movement. If she attempted to run, she knew that he would be after her like a cat after a mouse. She had no intention of trying to get away. All that mattered now was that she see Joshia.

Evie stopped at the foot of the staircase. She motioned with a hand. "You first. I'm not taking any chances with you. From now on, I want you to be where I can watch every move you make."

Marcia walked ahead of Evie, feeling the treads of the staircase beneath her feet. She wondered if Gregg had returned to the hideout and found her missing. Maybe he had been watching when Brock had caught her at the servants' quarters. What could he do with no weapon to defend himself? Yet she felt that Gregg would find a way to come to her.

At the head of the stairs, Evie suddenly grabbed her arm as they walked down the short hallway. "Just in case you get any crazy ideas."

"A lot of good that would do me," Marcia retorted.

Evie's face was a blank as they turned at the end of the hallway and started down the wide corridor to Joshia's room.

When they got to the door at the end of the corridor, Evie said, "I'll be watching you. Don't upset the old man. If you do, I'll punch you so fast it'll make your head spin."

With that, Evie opened the door and they walked into the room. Joshia was propped up in bed, his head resting on top of the pillows. His eyes were closed. Marcia once again felt her heart go out to that frail man who lay so quietly in the huge bed.

As they came nearer, Joshia seemed to sense their presence and his eyes opened. Evie was the closest to the bed and Marcia thought she detected a look of panic in his eyes. Marcia moved between Evie and Joshia, so that she was directly in his line of vision. The look of fear left his eyes.

Marcia said softly, "Don't worry, Mr. Spaniard. Everything is all right. Gregg is fine."

Evie was not looking, but Marcia saw Joshia's finger rise and drop on the crystal-white sheet. He had understood what she had said. Then his eyelids fluttered and closed.

"Okay," Evie said. "You've seen him. Now let's get back downstairs."

It was difficult for Marcia to walk out of the room and leave Joshia. He was so helpless. But then, she suddenly realized, so was she.

CHAPTER SEVENTEEN

It was as if she were sleepwalking, Marcia thought as she and Evie went down the staircase. She had a strange feeling that she would suddenly awaken and find herself back in her cozy bedroom in her apartment in Penwick—though, even as she took step after step, she knew that she was awake and that she was trapped at Windcliff.

"Like I said, the admiral's in good shape," Evie remarked as they reached the bottom of the staircase.

Not having an answer Marcia said nothing, although she wondered just how Joshia was actually feeling. This entire episode must surely have caused him anxiety. Not knowing where Gregg was and seeing such hostile and unfamiliar faces as Brock's and Evie's not to mention the surly Joe. Marcia wondered what thoughts were going on inside the mind of Joshia Spaniard.

When they entered the study, Marcia saw that Brock had prepared a platter of sandwiches.

"In case you get hungry," he said. "And how did you find the admiral? Evie has been taking good care of him."

"He appears to be just the same," Marcia said, declining Brock's offer of sandwiches. At the moment, food was the furthest thing from her mind. Besides, she knew that if she even took one bite of the food his hands had touched, it would stick in her throat.

Evie wasn't as particular as Marcia. She took a sandwich and sat down with it. Brock walked to the windows, where he paced restlessly.

"You're making me nervous," Evie said. "Why don't you sit down."

"Nobody's asking your opinion. So shut up," Brock snapped.

Marcia glanced from Brock to Evie. She could feel the tension like an electric wire in the study.

"Maybe your man Racon let you down. Maybe he isn't coming after all," Marcia said, adding fuel to the fire.

Brock whirled to face her. "And if you don't pipe down, I'll put a gag on your mouth!"

"Take it easy, Brock," Evie said. "She's just trying to get you all riled up. Can't you see that?"

Brock thought about what Evie had said and it seemed to quiet him down, although he still stood at the window.

"What if Racon has let you down," Marcia said. "What would you do then?"

"Racon isn't the only dealer around. If you have it in that pretty little head of yours that we're going to leave this island without the shipment, you've got another think coming."

There was a carafe of coffee on a desk near the wall. Marcia got to her feet, aware that Evie was watching her like a hawk. Marcia poured herself a cup of the hot, steaming liquid and returned to her chair. She warmed her chilly hands on the cup as she took a sip. Over the brim of it, she watched Brock as he gazed anxiously out the French doors.

Marcia wondered how near Gregg might be at this moment. If he had repaired the telephone wires, he might be in the kitchen placing a call to Penwick this very minute. Or he might have completed the call and was waiting for results. It was terrible not knowing where he was and what he was doing.

"Tell us, Brock," Marcia said, cutting through the silence of the room, "how did you happen to pick Teal Island for your business?"

"It was convenient. The goods were shipped to me from overseas. Joe and I picked them up and we spotted this island. It was a perfect setup. Isolated, yet near a small town where the authorities wouldn't be on their toes. I went to a bar in town and chatted with some of the customers. After a few free drinks, they were more than willing to tell me all I wanted to know about Teal Island.

"In an hour I knew everything there was to know about Windcliff. How Joshia had recently suffered a stroke. They even told me how many people worked here. A janitor at the hospital put me wise to Nurse Daniels. So by the time we came out to the island, we had done our homework. After that it was duck soup taking over. The element of surprise was on our side. All we had to do was flash our guns and the place was ours."

Marcia listened quietly, although inside she was livid with anger. She was glad that Gregg was not here. He would have jumped on Brock the minute he stopped talking.

"How did you know about me?" Marcia asked.

"Mrs. Holt let it slip that you were on the way. After a little prodding, we managed to get the whole story from Gregg before we locked him in his room."

"After which you began making plans about what to do with me. My coming here must have caused you considerable trouble."

Brock's anxious manner had disappeared. He was warming up to his subject. "At first, we were prepared to just be courteous and send you on your way. We hadn't banked on the storm, although there were warnings. When it looked as though you might be spending the night, I decided that it would be unwise for you to return to Penwick. Then, when you found the nurse's cap, I knew that you were becoming dangerous to our plans."

At that point Brock turned back to the window. He stood there, staring at something in the distance. Then he turned to Evie. "Stay here with Marcia. Joe's coming up the walk with someone. I'll have to find out who it is."

With that, Brock hurried from the study and went out of the house. Marcia wondered who the intruder might be. It most certainly wasn't Racon because Brock would have recognized him.

Whoever it was, Marcia thought, maybe he could help her. Yet the stranger might be a member of Racon's gang, someone Brock didn't know. Marcia tried to appear relaxed as she looked into Evie's watchful eyes. She knew that it was impossible now to convince Evie to leave Brock. As far as Brock was concerned, Evie was drawn to him hook, line, and sinker.

Evie took out another cigarette and lighted it. A blue cloud of smoke circled the chair where she was sitting.

"Kinda rough on you in the water last night, huh?" Evie said, and Marcia looked down at her wrinkled clothing. "You swam in all that icy water?"

"I had help, remember."

"Oh, yes. I keep forgetting about your boy friend."

"He's not my..." But Marcia didn't finish the sentence.

How could she deny what she felt for Gregg? Even if she had wanted to, she couldn't. Besides, Evie had already made up her mind about the relationship that existed between her and Gregg.

"You were saying?" Evie said as she blew a stream of smoke into the air.

"Gregg is a fine person. He helped me when I needed him most, when the boat was sinking. He cares deeply about his father. He's thoughtful, kind, and loyal. Which is something you can't say about Brock Janis."

Evie viciously ground out her cigarette. "Just watch what you're saying about Brock!"

"But it's true. How can you trust him? How can you love him, knowing what he's about to do?"

Evie looked disturbed for a moment. Then a look of indifference swept across her face. "Whatever Brock does is okay by me."

"How can you say such a thing?" Marcia said in disbelief. "Don't you care what happens to all those kids who get hold of that drug?"

"That's not my problem. That's theirs," Evie said coldly.

Marcia shivered at Evie's insensitivity. She only wished that Evie and Brock would be caught.

Suddenly, from the distance, Marcia could hear voices. She recognized Brock's mannered way of speaking and Joe's tough voice. There was a third voice, a familiar voice. Someone she knew from Penwick. Before she could put a name to the voice Brock walked casually into the study followed by Sergeant Farrell.

Marcia had known the police sergeant for years. She had gone through school with his daughter, Melinda. She felt a wave of hope surge through her as she looked into his jowly, pleasant face. Orley Farrell was a big man, as tall as Brock, and more muscular than Joe. He had a happy-go-lucky disposition and his face lit up with a broad smile when he saw Marcia.

"Glory be if it isn't little Marcia Carpenter. This place is just full of surprises."

"Hello, Sergeant Farrell. You can't imagine how good it is to see you." Marcia got to her feet, but as she made that move she saw a slight movement from Brock's jacket. He was getting a firm grip on his gun.

Marcia's eyes darted from the gun to Brock's face. The look in his eyes was one of cold menace. If she said anything wrong or made a false move, she knew that he would shoot Sergeant Farrell.

Quickly Marcia walked over to where the carafe of coffee stood. "Would you care for a cup of coffee, Sergeant Farrell?"

"Thanks, Marcia. I could use a cup," he said as he walked over to where Marcia tried to pour a cup with shaky hands. "Surprised seeing you here. Not to mention young Gregg's cousin. Where is Gregg anyway?"

Before Marcia could reply, Brock said, "He was called away to Boston. On business."

"I see," said Sergeant Farrell as he took the cup from Marcia.

"Didn't get your name?" he said over his shoulder to Brock.

"Janis. Brock Janis. And this is my fiancee, Evie Andrews."

"Pleased to meet you, Miss Andrews," Sergeant Farrell said, taking in Evie with a quick, appraising glance.

"Please sit down, Sergeant," Brock said, regaining his composure.

Sergeant Farrell glanced at Brock with a curious look, then turned his attention to Marcia. "How have you been, Marcia? Quite a surprise finding you at Windcliff. How long have you been here?"

Marcia told him about Adam Long. How he had asked her to deliver some papers and how the storm had kept her here. When she finished, she realized that there was some extra time unaccounted for.

"Marcia told us how she has always wanted to visit Windcliff," Brock said smoothly. "So we asked her to stay on for a few days."

"I see. That was very friendly of you, Mr. Janis," the sergeant said. "And how is Joshia feeling these days?"

Evie lit a cigarette and answered, "I've had some nursing experience and I've been taking care of him. He's about the same. Really too weak to have visitors."

"Since Nurse Daniels left so unexpectedly, it was a good thing that we arrived when we did," Brock said. "Uncle Joshia is doing as well as can be expected. He requested that the three of us remain here for the time being. My business allows me to have a flexible schedule."

Sergeant Farrell took a sip of coffee and looked at Brock. "What business are you in, if I may ask?"

Without hesitating, Brock said, "Import and exporting. My company is in Florida."

Sergeant Farrell nodded his head.

Brock directed a question to the sergeant. "May I ask what brings you to Teal Island? Is there anything I can help you with now that Uncle Joshia is incapacitated?"

"Just routine. I always check on Teal Island after a storm. Done it for years. Just in case there might be any trouble."

"That was good of you. But as you can see, we're getting along just fine. Marcia is a most welcomed guest."

Marcia bit her lip to keep from speaking out. Then,

in a controlled voice, she said, "How is Mrs. Farrell?"

"Chipper as ever. Still takes her four miles' walk every day, come rain or shine."

Sergeant Farrell settled back and began to extol the virtues of his wife. As he talked, Marcia glanced around the room. Brock and Evie were listening in a friendly, relaxed way. If she hadn't known better, she would have thought there was nothing amiss at Windcliff. This was the impression that Brock and Evie were trying to convey.

When Sergeant Farrell came to a break in his talk, Evie excused herself, saying that she really should check on Joshia, and left the room.

"Perhaps you should do some more work on the boat," Brock said to Joe, who grudgingly left the room, too. After he had gone, Sergeant Farrell said, "He's a quiet one."

"Joe? He's been with the company for years," Brock said. "I'll admit he isn't very talkative, but he does his job satisfactorily."

Marcia's mind was racing, trying to think of some way she could let Sergeant Farrell know what was going on. As long as Brock was here with the gun in his pocket, she couldn't say a thing.

When Brock offered more coffee, Sergeant Farrell got up and walked over to where his host stood. They both had their backs to Marcia. At that moment she quickly formed a plan. She reached for the pad and pencil and quietly tore off a slip of paper. She hurriedly wrote: *Send Help* on the slip of paper and shoved it into the mystery book that rested on the end table.

She glanced up and saw that Brock had been looking in her direction. Marcia prayed that he had not seen what she had done. He appeared not to have.

Sergeant Farrell returned to his seat and began telling Marcia all about Melinda and how she was doing in her job in Colorado. Even though Marcia was a bundle of nerves, it was good to hear about Orley Farrell's daughter. It was reassuring to know that outside these haunted walls life was going on as usual.

When Sergeant Farrell had run out of conversation and coffee, he got to his feet. "Everything appears to be in order here. So I'd better be getting back to the mainland. Nice meeting you, Mr. Janis."

It was now or never. Marcia kept her voice steady and calm. "Does Mrs. Farrell still read as much as she used to?"

Orley Farrell flashed her a wide, expansive grin. "Once she gets her nose in a book, she won't put it down until she finishes it. The house could be on fire and she wouldn't leave until she finished the chapter she had started."

"Oh, good. Why don't you take this mystery to her? I know she'd enjoy reading it," Marcia said, picking up the book and handing it to Sergeant Farrell. He didn't even glance at the title but tucked it under his arm.

"Thanks, Marcia. I'll return it when she finishes. Which will probably be about two hours after I hand it to her."

As he turned to leave, Brock brushed against the sergeant's arm and the book fell to the floor.

"I'm sorry," Brock said, crouching over the book. "That was clumsy of me."

Brock handed the book to the sergeant as Evie came back into the room.

After Brock and the sergeant had gone, Marcia returned to her chair. Evie sat opposite her, her face once more an inscrutable mask. As she placed a cigarette to her lips and flicked the lighter, Brock returned.

He walked over to Evie and held her hand so she could not extinguish the light. Then he held up a sheet of paper and touched it to the flame. Marcia saw her hopes go up in smoke as the paper caught fire.

CHAPTER EIGHTEEN

"A good try, my dear," Brock said as he scattered the ashes of the note into a turquoise-colored ashtray.

"What was that all about?" asked Evie.

"Marcia was trying to get help from the sergeant. She slipped a note to him in a book. Fortunately, I happened to see her."

Evie looked at Marcia, who returned a chilly glare of her own.

"She really has to be watched every minute," Evie said. "Maybe we should tie her up."

Brock thought about that for a moment, then said, "I don't think that will be necessary. We should be contacted by Racon any minute now."

"It can't be too soon for me. I can't wait to split from this place."

"Patience, Evie. Just keep thinking of all that money that will soon be ours. Imagine all the things you'll be able to buy with it."

This was too much for Marcia, all that gloating over the misery of others. "Aren't you both being a little premature? After all, the money isn't yours yet."

Brock's laughter was almost hysterical. "Just a matter of time, my little kitten."

"Racon's a trifle overdue, isn't he? Suppose something has happened to him?"

Brock found her words amusing. "If Sergeant Farrell is an example of the local police force, we have nothing to worry about on that score."

Marcia tried to keep her self-control. She felt her nails digging into the palms of her hands. If only Gregg would come. Had something happened to him? She wouldn't put it past Brock not to tell her if he had somehow succeeded in capturing Gregg. He was like an evil cat playing with a stunned mouse.

Walking over to the French doors, Brock opened them, letting in the warm sunlight and fresh air. The smoke from Evie's cigarettes had made the air in the room stale.

For want of something to do, not because she needed it, Marcia went over and poured herself a cup of coffee. As she poured the dark liquid, she thought about how close she had come to being freed from her captivity. If only Brock hadn't seen her slip that note into the book she had given Orley Farrell. She would have at least had that hope to cling to. Now that last hope of survival had been crushed by Brock.

Marcia was suddenly jarred from her reflections by the sound of whispering behind her. She pivoted and saw Brock bending close to Evie as he spoke in a hushed tone.

What was he planning now? she wondered. Was he hatching another plot with Evie? As she stood there, Brock became aware of her presence, and the whispering stopped. Evie turned her head toward Marcia and there was a mocking look in her eyes.

"Don't let me interrupt you," Marcia said as sarcastically as possible.

"You aren't," Evie replied. "Or couldn't."

With that Evie turned back and, holding Brock's face in her hands, kissed him with an intensity that made Marcia turn her head in embarrassment.

Marcia walked over to her chair, but she did not sit down. That seemed like all she had been doing for the past few hours. She sipped the coffee, but it had a bitter taste and she was tempted to toss it in Brock and Evie's faces.

Brock was now sitting on the arm of Evie's chair as he held one of her hands in his. No doubt Brock thought his affection appeared genuine. But it didn't. Marcia did not trust the man and neither should Evie. However, it was too late to tell Evie that.

"Tell me, Brock," Marcia said, facing him with a determined look, "what will happen to me and Joshia after you leave Teal Island?"

Brock feigned an innocent look. "Happen? Why nothing, of course. You will both be left unharmed."

"I don't believe you. We're both witnesses. If Joshia can't speak, I can."

Brock still remained unruffled. "By the time you're able to talk to the authorities, we'll be long gone. Now, why don't you just relax and forget about the whole thing? There is really nothing you can do about this situation."

Marcia put the cup down on the end table.

"I told you Brock isn't that kind of person," Evie said. "Now do you believe me?"

"I believe Brock will say anything, whether he means it or not," Marcia said coolly.

Evie leaned forward. There was a glint of anger in her eyes. "You'd better watch out what you're saying. For someone who's in the position you're in, you've got a pretty big mouth."

"That's why I can speak my mind. You don't for a moment think that Brock will let either Joshia or myself go free. Anymore than I believe that he intends to marry you."

Evie turned to face Brock, whose fingers had begun

to tap out a nervous staccato beat on the back of the chair.

"Well! What about it, Brock? Aren't you going to say anything? If you don't, then maybe I just might get to thinking that Marcia might be right."

Brock had become visibly shaken by this time. He had been put on the defensive and it was obvious he did not like that position. They began to argue violently. Seeing that they were unaware of her presence, Marcia slowly moved toward the open French doors. Brock and Evie were oblivious to her movements. Slowly she slipped through the doors and onto the short expanse of flagstone.

Once outside the room, Marcia broke into a run, heading toward the cliffs. Her only thought was to reach the hideout, to find Gregg. He had to be there. Otherwise he would have made an attempt to find her inside Windcliff.

The wind stung her face and whipped at her legs with unseen, razor-sharp fingers. Behind her, she could hear voices and shouts. Brock and Evie had discovered her absence. She had a head start, at least. Also, she knew where the hideout was and they did not.

Marcia had come to the end of the hedge that bracketed the garden. She turned onto the narrow pathway that would eventually lead her down to the cliffs. Her heart thudded inside her ears like a great drum and her lungs felt as though they had swallowed molten lava.

A gull swooped over her head and she dodged instinctively as it flew off toward the cobalt sea. In the distance, she could hear the murmur of the waves as they crashed relentlessly against the shoals.

The nearer she came to her pathway, the louder the

sound of the sea became. It roared, echoing against the hollows of the cliffs, drowning out the sound of Brock and Evie behind her. She dared not turn and see how close they were to her. She could not afford to waste one second in her flight. It would be too easy for her to slip or turn her ankle on the rocky trail.

Finally she arrived at the turn-off and spun to the right. The wind was even stronger now, carrying the salty taste of the sea water. Gregg would be there, he had to be! By breaking away and making her escape, she knew that she had all but signed her own death warrant. Brock was on the verge of completely shedding the veneer of gentility. He was ruthless. Now he had good reason to make certain she would never leave Teal Island alive. He could no longer pretend that he meant her or Joshia or Gregg no harm.

Marcia's legs were beginning to ache. It was all she could do to put one foot ahead of the other. She stumbled and sprawled across the trail. For a moment, she thought of giving up, just to be able to rest. Even though she knew that would mean that Brock and Evie would soon be upon her. From far away she heard the sound of rocks scattering on the trail from the cliffs beyond. With renewed determination, she staggered to her feet. As soon as she was up, she began running again.

Just that short break had helped. It isn't far, she kept repeating over and over to herself. She would soon be in the cave where she would be safe. Gregg would be there, she felt certain. He would meet her and hold her in his strong, tender arms, and she would be all right.

Now everything was familiar. There the outcropping of rocks which shielded the entrance to the cave. Marcia quickened her stride and made for the concealed entryway. Here she paused, hidden from view, and looked around. She could not see Brock or Evie. Had she finally succeeded in losing them?

She turned and walked into the dark tunnel that led to the depths of the cliff. Steadying herself with one hand that touched the cold granite wall, she weaved slightly as she headed toward the hideout. She could hear her quick gasps for air that echoed throughout the quiet passageway. Her legs had become shaky from all that running, but she still moved forward, determined not to rest until she found Gregg.

The stillness of the cave had a soothing effect on her nerves after the violent sound of the crashing of the waves. No longer would she think of the cave as a confining place. It was now a haven to her. She didn't even mind the dampness or the chill. Here she would be safe from Brock and Evie, the one place on the island where she need have no fear of being discovered.

Suddenly her hand touched openness and she knew she had arrived at the cave. By this time her eyes had grown accustomed to the murky gloom.

"Gregg! Gregg, are you there?" she cried out as she slipped from the tunnel into the room.

The only answer was her own voice that ricocheted against the gray walls of the hideout.

He has to be here, she said over and over to herself, as she fumbled for a match and brought light to the lantern. She held the lantern aloft in her hand as she peered around the now familiar room.

"Gregg! Gregg! It's Marcia. Where are you?" she cried in a voice that verged on hysteria. Still, there was no response to her pleas.

Marcia moved quickly around the hideout. Perhaps Gregg was injured and had crawled back to the cave and was too weak to answer her. As the lantern chased away the shadows, she explored every inch of the room and even ventured a way into the second tunnel that branched off from the cave. Finally she had to face the fact that Gregg was not there. Where was he?

She had come all this distance only to find that she had been mistaken. Gregg must be somewhere at Windcliff. Probably this very minute looking for her. Maybe she should not have made her escape. Yet she knew that she could not possibly have been able to remain in Brock and Evie's presence. Even though she did not know Gregg's whereabouts, at least, for the time being, she was safe from Brock Janis.

With a woebegone sigh, Marcia set the lantern on the rickety table and collapsed into a chair. Suddenly, she could not think anymore. A pervasive weariness engulfed her weary body. The walls of the cave appeared far away, hollow and lulling. It was as though she were adrift on a floating cloud of nothingness. She felt weightless and unable to fight this lassitude.

From faraway she could hear what sounded like footsteps, but she did not heed them. She could not rouse herself from this torpor, this consuming weariness.

Now she heard voices, distant at first, then gradually drawing nearer. She fought this unwanted lethargy and gradually felt herself responding. Suddenly alert, she sprang to her feet and whirled to face the entrance to the cave. In the flickering light cast by the lantern stood Brock and Evie. Brock was holding a gun in his hand.

"So this is where you and Gregg were hiding out," he said. "No wonder we couldn't find you."

"That was a good idea of yours, Brock. Letting her escape. You knew that she would lead us to this place."

So that had been Brock's plan, Marcia thought. And I was foolish enough to walk right into it.

"Unfortunately Gregg isn't here, too. Like Marcia I thought he would be waiting for her," Brock said.

Marcia was glad Gregg had not been here. Now she at least had the hope that he was free and would somehow come to her aid.

"This place gives me the creeps," Evie said with a shudder. "Let's take her and get out of here."

Brock hesitated. Marcia did not like the gleam in his eye. He was up to something and she had no idea what it might be. Maybe he intended waiting here until Gregg came, and then he would have the two of them. The gun in Brock's hand was steady, unwavering.

She was relieved when he said, "You're right. Gregg would be too smart to come back here. Come along, Marcia. And don't try anything."

Squaring her shoulders, Marcia walked toward them. Twice she had been captured and twice she had made her escape. But her luck might be running out.

As she passed Brock, he caught her arm in a firm grasp. "This time you won't get away. I'm going to stick by you like flypaper."

The walk through the tunnel was endless, hampered by Brock's restraining hold on her arm. His fingers dug into her flesh. She knew that her arm would be black and blue when he released his grip on it.

Evie complained all the way, saying that the island was a jinx and that the sooner they got off it the better.

Finally they were out of the tunnel into broad daylight. Evie walked ahead of them, with Marcia between her and Brock. When they got to the turn-off, she heard a muffled sound behind her and swirled to see Brock on the ground, the gun wrenched from his hand. Gregg grabbed the gun.

"Gregg! I knew you would come," she cried as he put his arm around her.

"I've been following and waiting for just the right chance to move in. I didn't want to take any chances that you might be hurt. Are you all right?"

"Now I'm fine. Oh, Gregg, I was so worried about you."

Gregg momentarily looked at her, and in that moment she saw the love she held for him returning from his dark eyes.

Gregg eased his arm from her shoulders as he nudged Brock with his foot. "On your feet, Cousin. We've got some walking to do."

At that moment Marcia felt something cold and hard press against the side of her head. She froze.

A harsh voice behind her said, "One move from you, Spaniard, and your girl friend's a goner."

CHAPTER NINETEEN

The voice belonged to Joe, who pressed the muzzle of his gun harder against Marcia's temple. She saw the surprised then concerned look on Gregg's face as he slowly let Brock's gun slip to the ground.

Immediately, Brock grabbed the gun and got to his feet.

"Sorry to disappoint you, Mr. Spaniard. You forgot there was a third member of our little group. Nice going, Joe."

Joe shoved Marcia forward and she fell into the arms of Gregg.

"They make a nice couple, don't you think?" Brock said in a teasing tone.

"All a matter of taste," was Joe's cryptic reply. "I saw what was going on. Racon made contact just a while ago and I was on my way to tell you when I saw you and Evie tailing the Carpenter dame."

At the mention of Racon's name, Brock's face suddenly took on a serious look. "Racon made contact. Good. Then we're ready to move the merchandise."

"It's about time," Evie said as she brushed a strand of hair out of her eyes. "Now maybe we can get off this crummy island."

"Is the boat ready?" Brock said to Joe.

Joe nodded. "All we have to do is get the stuff out of the cellar. After that, we should be at the mainland in less than an hour."

"You'll never get away with it," Gregg said.

Brock laughed. "We are getting away with it. As you can well see, Mr. Spaniard. I want to thank you for all the hospitality that you so graciously have shown me and my two companions."

"A nest of vipers would have been more welcome," Gregg said in disgust.

Joe made a move toward Gregg, but Brock held up a halting hand. "We wouldn't want to injure our host. Not just yet, anyway."

"What are we waiting around here for?" Joe said with a snarl. "Let's get that stuff out of the cellar."

Brock agreed and with Evie leading, and Joe and Brock bringing up the rear, they climbed the trail to the top of the cliffs.

As they walked, Marcia said to Gregg in a hushed voice, "Did you manage to fix the telephone wires?"

Gregg shook his head. "They did a good job on that. Spliced it and threw away the connecting wires. There wasn't any way I could repair them."

This was just another disappointment that Marcia had almost come to accept as the order of the day. So Gregg hadn't been able to contact the authorities at Penwick. There was no way now that they could expect any help from the mainland. She felt those watchful eyes on her back once more. Only, she knew this time who was watching her. Brock and Joe were right behind them.

When they got to the garden, Brock and Joe urged them on with a prod in the back with their guns. Walking toward the house, Marcia looked around at the garden and kept taking gulps of air.

She wondered if this would be the last time she and Gregg would ever see daylight. The thought of this made a quick shudder leap down her spine. She glanced at Gregg and was reassured by the firm way he held his chin. Gregg was not defeated, so Marcia took strength from him.

They entered the house through the kitchen door, where Brock halted them. He handed his gun to Evie.

"Keep this on them. If they make any effort to move, shoot. You know how to use the thing."

"Don't worry. But hurry it up, will you? I got a funny feeling when we were on the trail that we were being watched."

Brock sneered at her, "You're letting your imagination get the better of you. Who could be watching us?"

"I don't know. But the sooner we're out of here, the better I'll like it."

Joe had opened the door leading to the cellar. He hesitated on the top step, waiting for Brock to join him.

"In a way I'll be sorry to leave Windcliff. I've become quite fond of the old place," Brock said, looking around at the spacious kitchen. "However, as the saying goes, all good things must come to an end."

"Don't be too sure of that," Gregg snapped.

A sardonic smile crept over Brock's lips. "You can't tell me that you expect to have the posse come riding over the hills to the rescue. Come now, my dear Mr. Spaniard, the chips are down and you very well know it."

Gregg didn't appear to be intimidated by Brock's statement. "You seem very sure of that."

"Why not? We have the shipment. We have the guns. And we have you."

"What about us? You can't tell me that you plan on

just walking out of here and leaving us behind? I know you too well for that."

Brock's face did not change expression. Only his blue eyes shifted cunningly.

"You'll be taken care of. Come on, Joe. We have work to do."

With that Brock and Joe disappeared down the cellar steps. Marcia watched them go with a sinking feeling in the pit of her stomach. As long as they were delayed from their mission, she felt that Gregg and she still had time. Time for what? They had tried everything, but they were still in this terrible mess.

After they had gone, Evie stood with the gun on them. If Marcia had ever thought that Evie was just a poor, misunderstood person, she quickly changed her mind.

"This may take a little while. So you two sit down where I can see you," she said as she waved the gun in their faces.

They sat down on two chairs behind a deal table, Gregg opposite Marcia. Evie drifted over to a stool where she perched herself, the gun trained on them.

"I wonder how Dad is doing?" Gregg said. "You haven't seen him, have you?"

Marcia wanted to reach out and touch Gregg's hand. But she was afraid any unexpected movement on her part might alarm Evie.

"He's fine. I saw him earlier. I told him that you were okay and he seemed to understand."

"You're a wonderful person, Marcia. I feel terrible about you being dragged into all this."

There was nothing Marcia could say. She prayed that Gregg could read the understanding that flowed from her eyes to his. He nodded his head and looked down at his clenched fists.

It didn't take long for Brock and Joe to bring up their cache. They set it on the kitchen floor, then closed the door to the cellar. Brock looked down at the containers and there was a greedy gleam in his eyes.

"We'll soon be rolling in wealth," he chuckled.

"Not if we don't get this stuff to Racon, we won't," Joe said. "He can't wait forever, you know."

Brock glanced at Joe. "For this he can. We took all the risks. He can't continue his operation without us."

Evie slipped from her perch on the stool. She kept her eyes on Marcia and Gregg while she spoke to Brock.

"Why don't you get the big man here to help you load the stuff on the boat. Anything to get this show on the road."

"Good idea, my dear," Brock replied. "Pick up one of these containers and follow us."

At first Marcia thought that Gregg would refuse. She did not like the angry lines that were forming on his face. Yet she knew that he had no choice in the matter. Gregg got to his feet and picked up one of the containers.

"You come along, too, Miss Carpenter," Brock said. "It will be easier to keep an eye on you if we're all together. Besides, I wouldn't want to separate two lovebirds."

Gregg advanced menacingly toward Brock, but Evie was there with the gun.

"Easy there," Evie said as Gregg halted in his tracks.

The tension in the room was so thick, Marcia thought she could have cut it with a knife. She got to her feet as the three men walked out of the kitchen with the containers. Evie made a movement with the gun indicating that Marcia should follow them. She tentatively wondered if she dared take a chance on trying to wrestle the gun from Evie.

Evie was just her size, yet she was street-wise and Marcia knew that she would be on guard against any action she might take.

With reluctant steps, Marcia followed the three men from the kitchen. When they got to the hall, she couldn't resist glancing at the staircase and wondering how Joshia was doing. How little the frail man knew of what was going on downstairs. Yet, she thought, perhaps that was all to the good. If he had been aware, it would surely cause him great anxiety and possibly trigger another stroke.

They were going out the front door now. Marcia kept her eyes straight ahead. She did not want to look around at Windcliff, the house of her dreams. As she stepped across the threshold she was suddenly taken back to that rainswept afternoon she had arrived here. If she had known then what lay before her...That did no good, she thought. What was done was done. Besides, if she hadn't come, she would never have gotten to know Gregg. Would this be the last time they would be together? She quickly dismissed those thoughts for she still had hope.

The day was bright and clear now. The wind had lost its force, and in the distance the sea was dazzling with frothy whitecaps. She had never tired of that view from Penwick, nor would she ever tire of it from Teal Island.

They were taking the pathway that she had used the afternoon Joe had abandoned her. She knew now that it had been intentional on his part. He had wanted her to lose her way.

She was behind Gregg and her heart broke at seeing him being subjected to this final humiliation. If only he had managed to repair the telephone line. And if only Brock hadn't seen her slip that note to Sergeant Farrell.

They had reached the cliffs now and were starting to descend to the beach where their boat was moored. Each step that Marcia took was agony. She glanced back once only to be faced with Evie and the gun. Evie leveled the weapon at her and made a curt movement with her head.

As they walked down the pathway, Marcia once again sensed the eyes of the watcher. Had this sensation of being watched only been a figment of her imagination? Was it just her subconscious mind playing tricks on her? Whatever it was and whoever might be watching would be of no help to her now. In a short while the shipment would be on the boat. After that, it was anybody's guess as to what would happen.

The noise of the sea was deafening now that they were nearing the cove where the boat was moored. The runabout would be able to hold Brock, Evie, Joe, and the drugs, but it would be crowded. If she and Gregg were left alive, she only hoped that the boat would capsize and not make it to the mainland.

Arriving at the boat, they sat the containers on the ground, taking a moment to rest. Marcia glanced at Gregg and saw his eyes darting over the cliffs and into the hollows. She got the fleeting impression that he was looking for something. Then he turned his attention back to Brock.

"Why don't you let Marcia go? Send her back to the house to look after my father. I don't care what you do to me."

Brock's lips twisted in a mocking sneer. "Quite a noble gesture on your part, Mr. Spaniard. Unfortunately, you are in no position to do any bargaining. Both you and the girl will be taken care of."

"Wait a minute," Evie said, stepping close to Brock. "You promised me that you wouldn't harm anyone. Don't you remember?"

Evie reached out to touch Brock's arm. He shook off her hand with a quick twist of his shoulder. "My plans have changed."

"You can't do it," Evie said. "I won't let you!"

"I should let you have the same thing I'm going to give those two. After all, I don't need you anymore. I only brought you along so that you could take care of the old man. I was tired of you, anyway. All that talk about marriage."

Evie stared at Brock with a bewildered look on her face. "You mean, you aren't going to marry me? You knew that all the time!"

Brock's cold eyes stared down at her as though she were nothing. "What do you think? With you out of the picture, that would mean more of a cut for Joe and me."

Marcia felt a sudden surge of pity for the poor, gullible girl. She hadn't been able to see through that oily, sneaky character of Brock Janis. Evie sat there numb and confused. The wet spray from the sea had caused her makeup to run and she was a pathetic sight.

"You're a monster!" Marcia couldn't help but say, and Brock turned his cold eyes full upon her. "You'll never get away with this!"

"I'm afraid you're mistaken. I will get away with this. By the time your bodies are found, Joe and I will be out of the country. The authorities will never find us."

Gregg put his arm around Marcia and drew her close to him. Even at this dark moment he did not show any sign of fear. Marcia leaned her head against his strong shoulder and tried to let his courage seep into her own body.

"Let's get this over with." Joe's harsh voice split the air. "We've been fooling around long enough. What are you waiting for, Brock, an engraved invitation? If you won't do the job, I'll be glad to oblige."

Evie had inched across the rocky ground until she was right next to Gregg and Marcia. She no longer wanted anything to do with Brock. Too late she had seen what kind of a man he was.

Marcia saw that now she and Gregg and Evie had grouped together as Joe moved closer to Brock. As if by some unspoken thought they both raised their arms, pointing their weapons at the three huddled together. Overhead, a lone gull moved in an air current and the angry waves crashed against the rocks in the bay. Marcia braced herself, thinking this couldn't be happening.

Above the roar of the sea she heard a cracking sound and she saw the disbelieving looks on the faces of Joe and Brock as they crumpled to the ground.

CHAPTER TWENTY

They were suddenly surrounded by a horde of men; in the crowd Marcia saw the face of Sergeant Farrell. Gone was his usual happy-go-lucky attitude. His face reflected worry and concern, and when he saw Marcia standing there in Gregg's arms, the look was one of supreme relief.

"Darling, darling," Gregg kept repeating over and over. "It's all right now. Everything's all right."

Two of the men had lifted Brock and Joe to their feet. They hadn't been killed. Both Brock and Joe were still in a state of shocked surprise.

Sergeant Farrell walked over to where Gregg and Marcia stood. "You folks okay?"

"We're fine, Sergeant," Gregg said. "You arrived just in time."

"But how did you know we were in danger? Why did you come back?" Marcia gasped.

"I'll explain all that later. For now, why don't you two go back to the house. Gregg, you should check on your father and see how he's getting along. We'll take care of these people."

Marcia looked down at Evie, who was just sitting there staring as Brock and Joe were hustled away.

One of the men took her arm and helped her to her feet. Before he took her away, Evie turned to Marcia. "You were right about Brock all along. I should have listened to you."

Before Marcia could say anything, the burly man led Evie away. Marcia couldn't help feeling sorry for the pathetic creature who slouched down the beach.

"Come along, darling. Try to forget about all this," Gregg said as he turned Marcia toward the house.

They had little to say as they began the ascent to Windcliff. It was enough that they were still alive. The gratitude in their hearts was overflowing.

At the top of the cliff, they paused and looked down. Sergeant Farrell's boat had entered the cove and had anchored. From where they stood they could see Brock and Joe and Evie being taken aboard the craft. In a few minutes the boat cast off and headed toward Penwick.

"It all seems so unbelievable now that it's all over," Marcia said. "Like everything happened to someone else."

Gregg turned her away from the cliff and they headed toward the house. When they arrived at the portico, a heavyset woman with iron-gray hair and snapping brown eyes met them at the door.

"Thank heavens you're all right, Mr. Gregg," she said. "Carl and I were so worried about you. After that ruffian tied us up in the cottage, we didn't know what to think."

"We're just fine. Maggie Holt, I want you to meet Marcia Carpenter. Marcia has been through this whole ordeal, too, Maggie. She's got spunk."

Maggie Holt's eyes seemed to sparkle more and she smiled warmly at Marcia. "Pleased to meet you, Miss Carpenter. What a terrible thing this was. Who'd have thought something like this could happen?"

"How did you manage to get out of the cottage?" Gregg asked.

"Sergeant Farrell set us free. He and some of his men. He had to break down the door, I'm afraid, Mr. Gregg."

"Don't worry about that. Where is Nurse Daniels?"

"Upstairs with Mr. Spaniard. I do hope nothing has happened to him."

Gregg could see that Maggie Holt was about to break down. He very diplomatically said, "Do you think you might be able to fix all of us something to eat, Maggie? Marcia and I haven't had a decent meal in days."

This did the trick. Maggie was once more back on familiar ground. "Of course, Mr. Gregg. I'll just go and see what those ruffians did to my kitchen. Nice to meet you, Miss Carpenter."

Maggie hurried away as Gregg and Marcia entered the house. Without hesitating, Gregg headed for the circular staircase with Marcia at his side. The house had taken on a completely different atmosphere now that Brock and his cohorts were gone. Still, Marcia felt somewhat apprehensive as she and Gregg climbed the stairs. She realized this feeling sprang from her concern for Joshia. She prayed that he would be all right.

At the top of the staircase Gregg took Marcia's hand as they walked down the hallway to Joshia's room. The door was open and Nurse Daniels was bending over the bed. She looked up when Gregg and Marcia entered the room.

"How is he, Nurse Daniels?" Gregg asked in a low voice.

"He's doing just fine," Nurse Daniels said. "I was really worried about him all the time we were locked in that cottage."

Gregg took quick strides to the bed, where he paused and brought Marcia around so that Joshia could see her.

The old man's eyes were open and they were somewhat alert. The fear that Marcia had seen earlier when Evie had been in the room was gone. Marcia glanced down and saw that Joshia's finger had moved.

"I think he wants to tell us something," Marcia said.

Nurse Daniels started to speak, but Gregg silenced her. Then Marcia began to go through the alphabet. This time Joshia's responses were quicker, which sent a ray of hope through Marcia.

Gregg spelled out the words as Marcia went through the alphabet, with Joshia responding to the letter he wanted.

" 'Thank you,' " Gregg said as he put the letters together. "He said, 'Thank you.' He does understand."

"Praise be!" said Nurse Daniels.

Then Joshia's eyelids began to flutter and Nurse Daniels took charge once again. "I think you'd best go now. It looks as though Mr. Spaniard could use a little peace and quiet."

Before they left, Marcia leaned over and kissed Joshia gently on the cheek. Gregg took his father's frail hand and held it for a moment as the old man drifted off to sleep. Then they left the room. Behind them Nurse Daniels was tucking the blankets around the sleeping figure.

Closing the door, Gregg took Marcia into his arms. His mouth pressed against hers in a strong but tender kiss. Marcia felt herself responding warmly to his lips.

"That's for what you've done for my father," he said, and then he kissed her once again. "And that's for what you've done for me."

Later they were seated at the dining-room table with Sergeant Farrell. Maggie had brought in a platter of fried chicken with giblet gravy and a steaming tureen of succotash.

"You don't know how good it is to be back in my kitchen, Mr. Gregg," she said as she headed out of the room. She paused at the door that led to her domain and said, "I just hope those three get what's coming to them."

"Don't worry, Maggie. They'll be behind bars for a long time," said Orley Farrell.

It was Marcia who asked the first question. "There was another man. Someone they called Racon. He was their contact."

"He's in custody, too. Along with two of his cohorts. We've been keeping an eye on them ever since they came to town."

"Then you knew about Brock and the drugs all along," Gregg said.

"No. We were just suspicious of Racon and the way he was acting. He had rented an old shack down by the bay where I suppose he meant to stash the goods. You know how it is in a small town. Not much goes on that people aren't aware of. Especially strangers. We moved in on Racon, which isn't his real name, and found out what his game was. He was the contact man for the drugs and he was to signal Brock when it was safe to move the shipment."

Marcia finished swallowing a bite of chicken, then said, "But if you had arrested him, how did Joe get that signal that all was clear?"

"Racon told us what the signal was. I had one of my men send the signal after me and my men had landed on the island."

Gregg leaned forward with great interest. "You and your men have been here all the time?"

"Just a few hours. We couldn't move in because they had the drop on you. I was afraid that if we acted too quickly, either you or Marcia might be hurt."

Marcia took a sip of coffee as Orley Farrell made

swift work of a drumstick.

"May I ask if the men were with you when you arrived earlier today?"

Sergeant Farrell nodded. "I wanted to distract Brock and his gang while they came ashore and hid. After I left the men, I circled around, left the boat, and came ashore."

"Then it all started with Racon," Gregg said.

"Not exactly. I got a call from a friend of yours, Marcia. A woman named Clarita Hooper. She was worried about you. Had some kind of a story about watching you through her binoculars. Kept insisting you were in trouble."

Marcia sat back. Clarita Hooper, of course! The watcher of Windcliff! God bless her, Marcia thought to herself.

"At first I kind of ignored her," Orley Farrell went on, "if you can ignore someone like Clarita Hooper. I figured she just had an overactive imagination. Then, when I started thinking about Racon, I put two and two together and got you in a whole heap of trouble."

After that Sergeant Farrell told them how he had seen them being held at gunpoint on the trail and how he and his men had surrounded the house. As he concluded his story, Maggie came in with a dessert of fresh blackberries and whipped cream.

"This is too much, Maggie," Orley Farrell said.

"Come now. A big man like you ought to be able to put away a small bowl of blackberries."

As they were drinking their coffee after Maggie had cleared away the dishes, Marcia said, "You know I tried to ask you for help. When I offered you that book, there was a note in it. Just my luck that Brock had seen me write it."

Orley nodded. "That was why he jostled my arm

and knocked the book from under my arm. Even if I hadn't known what was going on around here, that book would have given me a hint."

"I'd hoped that your wife hadn't changed her reading habits," Marcia said.

Orley chuckled and scratched his head. "Not in twenty years. You knew as well as I did that she can't abide any kind of books but Westerns. And here you slip me a mystery story!"

Everybody had a good laugh. Marcia realized that this was the first time she had heard laughter in Windcliff since she had been there. Oh, Brock had laughed, that was true. But his laugh was dark and diabolical.

"Guess I'd better be getting back to Penwick," the sergeant said. "It looks like I have a long night ahead of me. If you like, I'll take you back with me, Marcia. My boat should be back by now."

Marcia suddenly realized there was no reason for her to remain now that Brock and Evie and Joe were no longer holding her captive. She looked across the table as Gregg folded his napkin.

Before she could answer, Gregg said, "Thanks anyway, Sergeant Fa rrell. But Marcia and I have some unfinished business. I'll see that she gets safely home."

After Marcia and Gregg had seen Orley to the door, Gregg said, "Now for that unfinished business."

"Yes?" Marcia said expectantly.

"You did bring some papers for me to sign, didn't you?"

Marcia stared at him for a second in disbelief. Was he serious?

"If you wait in the library, I'll get them," she said, trying to keep the annoyance out of her voice. "I left them in my room."

"Don't take too long. I'm a very impatient man," Gregg said as Marcia headed toward the staircase.

She wondered if Gregg was only teasing her, or if the papers were really the unfinished business he had spoken about.

How well do I really know Gregg Spaniard? she thought as she went to her room and picked up the documents. After all, we were thrown together by circumstances and now those circumstances have been changed. Her business was finished at Windcliff.

Yet as she walked down the staircase, she could still feel his arms around her and recall the loving way he had called her darling. Had he really meant what he had said, or was that just a word he hadn't even been aware he had uttered?

Gregg was sitting in a chair at the desk when Marcia entered the library.

"That didn't take long," he said.

"You gave me the impression that you were anxious to sign these," Marcia said, not able to keep the chill out of her voice.

"Indeed I am. Please sit down. I'll only be a moment."

Marcia sat quietly by the window. She could not get over the sudden change in Gregg. Here he was all business, as if nothing had happened. She tried not to look at him, forcing herself to stare out the window. But she saw nothing—only the blur from the unwanted tears that clouded her eyes.

Don't be such an idiot, Marcia Carpenter, she chided herself as she blinked back the tears. In a little while you'll be gone from Windcliff. Whatever happened here will just be a memory. You'll go back to the office and Gregg will have his hands full managing Windcliff and the various family businesses.

Thinking of the office, she wondered if Adam had returned from New York. Try as she might, somehow the office or Adam or Pen wick just didn't seem awfully important.

Gregg's voice brought her out of her reverie. "Good. Everything seems to be in order. Now, as to the matter of your fee..."

Marcia could not believe what she was hearing. Gregg had reached into a drawer of the desk and was fumbling around.

"It isn't necessary that you pay me, Mr. Spaniard," she said, rising to her feet. "Adam Long pays me a very adequate salary."

Gregg appeared to be ignoring her protest. "That's all very well and good. But I insist upon you accepting this."

Gregg had risen from the desk and was walking toward her. There was a strange look in his eyes. Marcia could not fathom what lay in their dark depths. She only knew that Gregg Spaniard was a disappointment to her.

Gregg reached out and took one of her hands in his. She tried to draw it away but he held it tightly. Then he turned her hand over slowly and gently slipped a ring on her third finger.

Marcia looked from the ring to Gregg. His eyes were warm, and there was tenderness in them that brought a lump to her throat.

"It was my mother's. It was worn by my father's bride. As I would wish you to wear it as my bride. Will you, Marcia?"

Her answer was lost as she flung herself into his

waiting arms. His kiss was demanding yet strangely gentle. When they parted, Marcia looked at the narrow band of gold that caught the sunlight.

"Yes, I'll marry you, Gregg. I've loved you for a long time."

"And I you," Gregg said as he kissed her once more.

"But there are a few things I have to take care of in Penwick first," she said.

Gregg cocked an eyebrow. "Such as?"

"Turning in my resignation. Packing a few things. Closing up my apartment."

Gregg laughed. "Of course. We'll do that together."

As they started toward the door, Marcia said, "And one very special gift I have to buy."

Gregg looked at her in puzzlement. "What is that?"

"The finest pair of binoculars I can find for Clarita Hooper."